Rivals

ML PRESTON

Rivals
Copyright © 2019 by ML Preston
ALL RIGHTS RESERVED
Published by ML Preston
Cover Design by T.E. Black Designs
Edited by StudioEnp

No parts of this publication may be reproduced, stored in a retrieval system, or transmitted in any form or by any means, electronic, mechanical, photocopying, recording, or otherwise, without the prior written permission of the copyright owner.

This book is sold subject to the condition that it shall not, by way of trade or otherwise, be lent, resold, hired out, or otherwise circulated without the publisher's prior consent in any form of binding or cover other than that in which it is published and without a similar condition including this condition being imposed on the subsequent purchaser. Under no circumstances may any part of this book be photocopied for resale.

This is a work of fiction. Any similarity between the characters and situations within its pages and places or persons, living or dead, is unintentional and co-incidental.

This book contains mature content, including graphic sex. Please do not continue reading if you are under the age of 18 or if this type of content is disturbing to you.

CHAPTER ONE

I woke this morning excited and nervous about a meeting with my boss, Mr. Armstrong. He sent an email yesterday as I was leaving. It was cryptic, and even though I know my performance isn't an issue, I'm a little concerned. With all the different companies laying people off, job security is a real thing. I rolled out my yoga mat early this morning for a some meditation and relaxation before heading to the office. No reason for me to go in there tense. One thing has me worried—my co-worker, Lucas Weathers. The sound of his name sends icky feelings through my body.

"Good morning, Simone," my assistant, Tanya, says when I step off the elevator.

"Hey, Tanya. Has Armstrong made an appearance yet?"

"Why don't you ask Armstrong yourself, Ms. Greene,"

a boisterous voice says from behind me. Mr. Calvin Armstrong, CEO of Merit Investment Firm, a company started by his great-grandfather.

I turn to greet him and extend my hand for a shake. "Mr. Armstrong, good morning. I was about to come to your office for our scheduled appointment."

He takes my palm into his strong, yet delicate chocolate grasp, reciprocating the gesture.

"Were you now? I just saw you arrive."

"Well, yes. I was going to put my stuff down and..."

"Save it, Greene, and meet me in my office in five."

He walks the opposite direction from which I stand, and all my destressing goes out the door.

"Tanya, please hold all my calls and pray I have a job when I come out of his room."

"Got it," she replies.

I quickly retreat to my work space and put my personal things away and then head to his office. I stroll down the corridor, passing by my nemesis' spot along the way. *Look at him. So smug, and cocky, and oh my god is he arrogant.* He and his team are apparently having a good laugh about something when he catches wind of the mean eye I'm sending him.

"Good morning, Simone," he says.

The others fall silent and swivel in my direction. In true Simone Greene fashion, I roll my eyes and continue my journey.

"Hi, April. I'm here to see Mr. Armstrong," I say to his secretary when I reach his location.

"Oh, yes. Go right on in, Simone. He's expecting you," she replies.

I enter Armstrong's territory, and he gestures for me to take a seat while he finishes up a call. No matter how many times I've been in his office, I always take a few moments to glance at the accolades he and his family have accumulated over the years.

He places the receiver on the base and turns to me. "Simone, can I get you something to drink?"

"Um, no, sir, thank you."

"Very well. Are you familiar with Clemet Industries?"

"Yes, I am. I've studied their business profile for the past year. They've had some strong surges in the market recently."

"Yes, Greene. You are very studious and always on top of the movers and shakers. One of the many reasons why I hired you." Just then his door swings open, and in walks *him*. "Right on time, Weathers. Have a seat."

He takes the chair beside me, and I have to fight the hurl that is forming in the bowels of my stomach.

"Simone, you look nice today," Lucas says, trying to goad me.

I don't buy into his nice guy façade and turn my attention back to Mr. Armstrong, who can obviously sense or even feel the tension between us. I can tell by the sharp glances he throws among the two of us.

"So, as I was saying, the company has been approached to take on Clemet's financial account and help them move the money around. Invest smartly and show them where they can afford to take risks and not bankrupt the company. I like the chances of bringing them on board, but I know it would be all but confirmed if one of you leads the charge. Both of you show strong management skills and you know the clients' likes and dislikes. I like those who do their homework, and with the amount of knowledge you've each demonstrated for Clemet, I trust either of you will excel with this account. It's for those reasons, this choice hasn't been simple to make, so we'll need to take a different approach. Each of you will put together a pitch, one that can be presented to Clemet Industries as a fully loaded proposal to maximize their bottom line and increase their income. If you get the contract, and do it right, there may be a promotion waiting."

"Mr. Armstrong, you know I'm the best person for this account," I say confidently. The thought of having to compete for an account against Lucas irritates me. He has won some big clients, but I question his methods.

"Again, you both are my top managers, so I can't make this decision lightly. You two will have to bring your A game. I have a meeting scheduled with them at the end of this week, so I expect the proposals in my office no later than Friday afternoon."

"Friday? Like tomorrow or next Friday?"

"Tomorrow. Is that something you can't handle, Ms. Greene?"

I never want to look incompetent in front of my boss, and certainly not Lucas. But I'd prefer a little more time to develop and do my research. I glance at Lucas, who is wearing a smirk I want to slap off his face. "I can handle it, sir," I reply, my gaze locked directly on to his. He will not intimidate me.

"Great. Now off you two go. Good luck to you both."

We stand to exit, and Lucas steps aside, opening the door, being all chivalrous and shit. I can't even muster up a thank you and storm out, heading straight to my office.

"Are you such a bitch you can't even say thank you?" he asks, keeping up with my stride.

"Are you are such a kiss-ass you had to weasel your way into Armstrong's plan. You know he wants me to have the client."

"Oh, really? Why? Because you went to school at his alma mater?"

Throwing personal jabs is not what we need to do in front of everyone, but he crossed the line. "It's better than fucking his daughter. In his house. In his bed."

"How'd you find out?"

"Word gets around, Mr. Weathers." I reach my office but stop at the threshold, not allowing him to enter. "If I were you, I'd secede now. It'll be less painful," I say when I turn and face him.

"But I like pain, Ms. Greene."

"Good. Then this should please you well." I slam the door, and it barely misses his mug...barely. Through the folds of the blinds on my window, I see him walk away with his hand rubbing at his nose. Taking a couple of deep breaths, I sit and begin to strategize how to win the Clemet account. I pull up the company's website and launch researching the board of directors and putting together a cheat sheet. After all, they are the ones who influence a company's financial decisions. This is going to be tougher than I thought. Some of the more influential members are into the adventure sports sort of thing, so I can't do a lunch with them tomorrow at a racetrack. Too short notice. I see a few of them love golfing so I figure a lunch at the local country club would be perfect. *I golf a little. Putt-Putt counts, right?*

"Tanya, can I see you for a moment?" I mutter through the intercom.

"Yes, Simone," she says, entering my office.

"Can you call White Barn Country Club and set up a nine-hole with lunch for me tomorrow. Make it for four people."

"Okay, but Weathers has a time scheduled already. Belle already put it on the office schedule."

I roll my eyes, and for a moment, I can't get my lids to reopen and think they may have finally stuck. "Perfect. Book it thirty minutes before his, but don't put it on the calendar. I'll draft the invite for you to send to the team over at Clemet's so you can coordinate with their assistant.

Also, call HR and schedule me off work tomorrow for business."

"Okay, got it, boss lady. Anything else?"

"I hate to imposition you, but if you hear anything from Belle, Lucas' assistant, let me know. I want to stay one step ahead of him. We meet with Armstrong and the team Friday morning, and I want him to eat shit."

"I'll do what I can." She leaves, closing the door behind her.

Online, I find me some gear for tomorrow and order several of my bi-fold brochures for pickup at the local print supplier. When I complete my research, I go to our supply closet for promotional material to take to my luncheon tomorrow. When I swing open the door and find—*HIM*—in there grabbing the same items.

"Great minds do think alike, I see," he mutters.

Taking a deep breath, I reluctantly enter the closet. Once inside, I select some folders, pens, our company brochure, and a few fun things like stress balls while working to keep from showing my disdain. Not very effective, I'm sure, because I feel his eyes on me.

"What did I do to you, Simone, that you won't even talk to me? We're colleagues whether you like it or not."

"Doesn't mean I have to speak to you."

"True, but you don't even try."

"Lucas, I don't like you." I continue to grab things and toss them into my bag.

"Throw me a bone and tell me why?"

I refrain from my usual expression of disgust and turn to face him. "You're cocky."

"Confident," he corrects.

"Like I said, *cocky*, arrogant, egotistical, conceited, self-righteous, and a douchebag. You come in here and magically make your way up to the top ranks and haven't put in nearly half the work I have to attain my position. I guess fucking the boss's daughter has its privileges. Oh, wait. Maybe it's a different kind privilege."

"I know you're not playing the race card. Our boss, the CEO, the lineage of this company, is African-American, so race doesn't apply."

"No, but sexism does."

"You honestly think Carver Armstrong would be a person of that caliber?"

"No, but you would. You'd play any card to get what you want. But this will be a battle you will not win." I open the door and find people scurrying around trying to appear busy when you know damn well they were eavesdropping.

My email tone goes off, advising my order is ready for pickup. I return to my office and schedule a team meet up for brainstorming and fact gathering. We meet in the conference room that unfortunately puts me in the path of *him*. As I casually stroll by his office, I see he, too, has assembled his staff. They are laughing and having a grand time. I mean, why is he even competing for this account? Look at him, just smug, and cocky, and overconfident.

Armstrong knows this should be *my* account. Lucas catches me glaring, and I flip him the bird while I continue to my destination.

"Okay, what do we know about Clemet?" I ask, starting the impromptu agenda while my team settles down.

"They're a startup software company and have amassed millions in the last quarter since their IPO went public," Deshaun says, beginning the round of fact revelations.

"Specializing in security software for schools ensuring predators aren't able to access the information on children and cross-referencing it with social media accounts to find their targets," Terri adds.

"Yeah, they also work with hospitals to help encode the sensitive health records as well," Roshanda continues.

While the information is shared, I take notes and use my tablet to pull the facts and highlight the points sharing them on the drop-down overhead. "Okay, these are a good start, but what about the founding member or members? What do we know about them? I mean, I know a few of them are adrenaline junkies, and some golf, which is why I'm going to hit a few balls when I leave." I get smiles for my last comment.

"Leo Rauch is the founder and president of the company. He maintains a hands-on approach, not wanting to see his ship sink if he left all decisions in the hands of his board, which is also his family. His wife, Janelle, sons

Toddrick and Leo, daughters Ayanna and Kristen head up the directors, but they have others as well," Manny adds to the discussion.

"Good intel. Family man, family-run business. That lets me know he takes his company and money very serious, and for us to manage their investments is gaining a big trust factor."

We brainstorm ideas and even do a mockup of what we should emphasize during my presentation tomorrow. I send a few people out to gather industry bites about the company and get some real-time quotes from a few the users of their product. We are working at a good pace when the door suddenly pops open, grabbing my attention.

"Excuse me, but are you going to hold your little meeting any longer? I need the conference room." Lucas asks annoyingly.

"You have some nerve to barge in here like you own the place, Lucas. Go use the conference room down the hall. It's available, and I'm working."

"Yeah, it's closed for an air conditioner issue. So, you need to pack up, Greene."

There are times when I can keep the craziness down. This isn't one of those times. "You have the fucking audacity to interrupt my meeting and then talk shit to me in front of my team, our colleagues, like it ain't nothing? If you don't get the fuck out of here, Lucas…"

"Oh, so what, are you threatening me? Go ahead, try me."

He encroaches my personal space, the one thing that pushes me overboard. I draw back to hit him, and my hand is caught by my assistant.

"Stop it, you two. Why are y'all always going at each other's throats?"

"Umm, Armstrong is heading this way, and he looks pissed," Janice says.

For the sake of my job, and I'm sure *he* was thinking the same, we all scramble and make it look like we were leaving and his team is settling in for their meeting. I need the fresh air anyway.

"What the hell is all the screaming down here? Sounds like my kids when they were growing up."

"Oh, we're sorry. We were having team Lucas and team Simone battle cheers. You know, like in high school. Good ol' team spirit." Even I didn't believe it, but I had to spin it. It's no secret we don't get along.

"Yeah, Mr. Armstrong. Simone here is a real screamer. Did you know she was captain of her squad in high school?" Lucas says while he snakes his arm around my shoulders like we're friends or some shit.

"Very well. Be sure to keep it at a minimum."

He turns and walks back to his office, and when he gets out of earshot range, I stomp Lucas' foot and get right in his face.

"Don't fucking touch me ever again!" I grab my things from the conference table and walk back to my space.

"Whew, that was close," Tanya says when she enters.

"The absolute nerve of him. I mean, he interrupts my meeting, demands we leave, and then...touches me. Like, the balls on that fucker are huge." I pace incessantly, trying to calm down but find myself becoming more enraged. "How does he think it's okay for him to just...ugh. I need to get out of here before I break something. Call me on my cell if you need me." I pack up my bag and head out to cool off and do more research—i.e. go to a driving range—and then head home.

CHAPTER TWO

My friends, Hailey and Natalie, join me in my quest to be able to at least tee off. We arrive at the facility, purchase our buckets of balls, and go to the range.

"So, let me get this straight. Your boss is eyeing representing a large software company and has forged a competition between you and your rival to see who gets the account?" Natalie quizzically states.

I swing my iron and strike the ball forcefully. "Yep. That's the plan." I peer out at the green to see how far my orb traveled so I can mark my card.

"And you're out here playing golf with us?" Hailey asks, same tone.

"Yes. Why?"

"I would be researching or spying on his plans instead of hanging out with us," Natalie comments.

I tee up and take another swing. "This is my plan. I have a meeting with them tomorrow at the country club, so I needed to see if I remembered anything my dad taught me."

"Okay, so what's his angle?" Hailey responds.

I pull back and swack the next ball before answering. "Oddly enough, the same. Tanya told me today as she was scheduling our meeting. But then the fucker interrupted my time with my team and demanded I leave the conference room. I mean, this asshole acts like he runs everything. I can't stand the ground he walks on." I take a swing and hit the ball past the green. I'm sure someone's car is dinged.

"Um, I think you need to grab a drink to calm your nerves. Let's put the club away and go have a seat," Natalie says, removing my golf equipment from my hands.

Maybe she's right. I am too worked up. Even a few of the men standing nearby move away when we head inside to the bar, probably to avoid my wrath. The girls snag a table by the window closest to the entrance so we can watch the guys as they come in. After a few rounds of cosmos and margaritas, it's safe to say I'm completely relaxed.

"Wow, he's handsome," Hailey says when a tall, tan, brown-haired gentleman walks by our table, passing us a subtle yet sexy smile.

I catch another look at him and make eye contact

while slowly sipping my drink. He assumes that's an invitation to strike up a conversation.

"Ladies, good afternoon. May I buy another round for the table?"

"Yes, you may, suga. My name is Natalie. This is Hailey and Simone."

He extends his hand and takes ours into his palm when we are introduced.

"Pleasure to meet you all. My name is Jesse Cetera. Mind if I join you? I'm meeting my friend here for a short game."

"Please, have a seat." Natalie scoots over abruptly and bumps into me.

My friends are all about dating. Me, not so much. My career is the only thing occupying my time. I notice a faint tan line on our guest's ring finger and roll my eyes listening to him make empty promises while he flirts with my friend. He catches me looking, and a streak of red colors his cheeks. Soon a tall, sun-kissed ebony man calls his name as he approaches our table.

"Jesse," he says, his voice a little amplified.

Now this is a drink of water I can partake. I straighten up and arch my back slightly and prepare for a round of introductions.

"Hey, Harlan, you made it. Meet Natalie, Hailey, and Simone. Ladies, this is my brother-in-law, Harlan."

Brother-in-law? I put the girls back to their resting position when I shake his hand.

"Ladies, it's a pleasure to meet you all. Let me get another round." He raises his hand for the server's attention.

"Uh, I think I've met my limit. I'm going to head home and get my research done. You ladies enjoy your time. I'll catch up tomorrow after I land this account."

Hailey stands to let me out of the booth seating, and we say our goodbyes. "I can't believe I was about to put myself on display to get the attention of a man," I say to myself when I enter my car. I shoot Natalie a text to advise of the wedding ring tan line I saw, letting her know to be careful with that guy before I pull off and go home.

I stayed up late working on this project. Tanya came by with wine and snacks to help me pull it all together. To thank her, I gave her the morning off so she could sleep in. Meanwhile, I grab a coffee with a triple-shot of espresso to help me at least function during the golf course meeting. Gaining their trust before I pitch my proposal is imperative if I want to win this account. To give us enough lag time for an actual discussion, I didn't book a normal game. Only a few putting rounds. After introductions and speaking with Janelle and two other board members, I changed a few things around and reprinted it for my presentation when I returned to the office. I say a quick prayer and walk over to meet Armstrong where my rival is sitting outside waiting to go in. Taking the seat next to him, I pray he doesn't speak to me.

"Good luck in there, Simone."

So much for wishful thinking. I choose a vow of silence, he scoffs a bit at my unreturned gesture. The door opens, and Armstrong appears with a smile on his face. I straighten up, putting my bitter bitch attitude aside.

"Mr. Armstrong, good afternoon," I say, shaking his hand.

Lucas follows with his own platitude, and we are ushered in to the office.

I deliver my proposal, which is a knockout punch to my competition. Focusing on the reason he started this company, which was the attempted abduction of his daughter, and the lack of protocols in place in schools today to prevent personal information from becoming public knowledge. How a person can learn a child's schedule and plan their attack. This seemed to drive great interest from those in attendance. I also share stories of school officials who were able to partner with law enforcement and track down potential threats discreetly. Wrapping up my pitch, I take my seat and listen as Lucas presents his. Sweat forms on my palms, and I swallow several times when he lists a few cost points I missed during my research. I compose myself, refusing to let that be a factor. When he finishes, we're both dismissed while they discuss the presentations.

The afternoon crawls along, and I continuously buzz

Tanya to see if she's heard anything. I even take my shoes off so I won't wear the soles down from my pacing.

"You know, maybe if you want to relax a bit, go fake nice with Lucas so there won't be any hard feelings when it is announced who will manage the Clemet account," Tanya suggests as she brings me my mail for the day.

I won't even take calls until I find out my fate. Looking at my calendar, I realize I have to pick my mother up from the airport tomorrow. With all the events over the past day, it slipped my mind she's visiting. I haven't seen her since she went on her singles cruise a few months ago.

"I don't know. You think that'll help?"

"Just clear the air. At the end of the day, one of you will not get it. No need to gloat. Be humble."

Fuck, I hate when she's right. I take a deep breath, slide my heels back on, and go to Lucas' office to make *nice.* "Hey, Weathers, I stopped by to wish you good luck. May the best person win."

"Oh, I will, and then take a partnership leap over you."

One thing that pisses me off is arrogance. I'm trying to be the bigger person, but he always manages to bring the mean girl out of me. "All I wanted to do is come clear the air between us, but your pompous ass can't even allow it to happen. So, you know what, fuck you, Lucas."

"Really, Simone? Fuck me. You wish I would even let you get close enough to see what it's like to fuck me, so fuck you. With your snobbish ass."

"Oh, I'm a fucking snob? I'm not the one driving

around in an extension of my penis, you pretentious asswipe."

Our argument becomes so heated, I don't realize we have the attention of the entire office, including Mr. Armstrong and our beloved guests, until Armstrong politely shouts, "In my office, NOW!"

I shake my head as I saunter off to his office to get my immediate pink slip and Lucas follows. Why do I let him get under my skin? Mr. Armstrong is a very calm man, but the look in his eyes would give cyclops a run for his money.

"In all my years, I have never seen such an outrageous display of unethical, unprofessional behavior than what you two have showed here today. I am outright appalled. My two top managers going at each other like a pack of ravenous wolves."

"I'm sorry, Mr. Armstrong. I allowed my passion to rule me instead of keeping a cooler head."

"Yeah, me, too. I goaded Simone and I shouldn't have."

"I appreciate you for admitting your failures. But nonetheless, the damage has been done. Both proposals were good, but unfortunately, Clemet's accounting was here and witnessed the blowout. They are impressed with our offers and reputation but simply do not have the trust in the professionalism we promised. I hate to have to say this, but neither of you get the account. I'll have to give it to Edwards."

"But—" I try to interject, but it's immediately shot down.

"I don't want to hear it. You bought this on yourself. Be glad we didn't lose the contract completely or we'd be having an entirely different conversation. I will say, Simone, your proposal was the one they were going to go with, so Edwards will use it to model his strategies. I'll make sure you get a portion of the bonus associated but no credit. We won't even talk about your promotion probability. For either of you. You are hereby placed on a thirty-day notice to clean up your act and work together without killing each other. You are dismissed."

Lucas blows right past me, and I fight to hold back my emotions. Closing the door as I enter my office, I sink in my chair and let out low, inaudible sobs. I was such an idiot falling for his trap. I clean my face and pull up the accounts I do have and check on their performance. Throughout the rest of the day, I work to keep my sanity. I'm so glad it's Friday, because I need to go get a drink and put this week behind me.

CHAPTER THREE

I decide to go to the bar down the street from the office for two reasons: One, I can walk there after work, and two, leave my car safe and secure in the parking garage in case I have to take an Uber home. I trek into the crowded bar searching for a place to sit and wallow in my despair. Not a single table was available. Groups of people gathered for happy hour fill the spaces along the perimeter while the center has a few high tables and a good-sized section for dancing, leaving me to survey the bar area in hopes to find a seat and not conversation. My scan is halted when I find a vacant barstool, but sitting right beside it is my rival, Lucas Weathers. I contemplate leaving and calling it a day since I have plans with my mother tomorrow, but the weight of disappointment is too heavy to cast aside. I swallow my pride and casually walk towards the empty seat. Upon my approach, I see Lucas has two empty glasses in front of him and is nursing a third.

"I'll have a double vodka with a twist of lime and splash of cranberry juice," I say to the bartender.

The tall, slender, and attractive young woman prepares my cocktail and places it in front of me. The first sip is to make sure it's right, the second one is to begin my meditation, followed by a deep sigh.

"Your proposal was really good, if I may say," Lucas speaks before pulling another sip from his glass.

I could be the catty bitch he's used to, but considering all that transpired today, I choose not to. "Thanks. Yours was quite amazing. You hit points I forgot to mention." I reply.

"Who the fuck are we kidding, they both were. But Armstrong gives it to—"

"Paul- Fucking-Edwards!" I exclaim, my face distorted with disgust.

We look at each other and burst out in loud laughter. I finish off my drink and call for a refill.

"Here, let me get that," Lucas interrupts. "You know what, put all drinks on my tab. We have a lot of talking to do."

The bartender looks to us and offers a smile, but my look to her is anything but complimentary.

I turn to my adversary and ask for an explanation. "So, what do we have to talk about?" I take a sip of my drink and give my thumbs-up.

"Simone, why do you hate me so much?" he retorts, wasting no time jumping into the fire.

"I don't *hate* you, per se. I just strongly *dislike* you."

"Okay. Why?"

"You walk around like you are the king of money management, and your mere arrogance repulses me." I down my drink after I lay my words on the table and call the bartender for another. After all, he's paying.

"Ouch. Save some of my heart for me, Greene. Shit." He chortles.

"I'm sure you have some not-so-nice words for me."

"Nope." He swallows the last of his drink and signals for a refill.

"Oh, come on. We go at each other like champion fighters. Certainly, you have something to say." I partake my drink and wait for his reply.

Silence falls between his lips, and when I look at him, his gaze is fixated on me. His eyes are soft, and I notice the tone of bright gray that reflects in his pupils. He has scruff adorning his well-chiseled jawline, and his hair is not its usual coiffed style. *Has he always been this fine,* I think to myself? A rush of heat overtakes me, and I stand to pull my cardigan off. The straps of my bra and cami fall from my shoulder, and out of instinct he assists with helping them up. The soft touch of his fingers mingling with my warm brown skin sends electrifying pulses through my body. He's slow to remove his hand from its place and flashes a shy smile when he does.

"I'm sorry. I saw the straps fall and didn't want you to have an embarrassing wardrobe malfunction." He chuckles a bit, and I cast him a smile. "Oh, she can be soft, and she has a beautiful smile."

"Oh, wow. Flattery? That's how you come for me?"

He declines to respond, but there is something sexy and inviting in his eyes. "I tell you what. Let's play a game," he requests.

"What kind of game?" I ask, tilting my head to the side in an inquisitive manner.

He signals for the bartender.

"Ready for another round?" she says upon arrival.

"Bring me two shot glasses, a fresh chilled bottle of Patron, a tray of limes, and salt."

I look at him quizzically but intrigued, nonetheless. "Ooo a shot game." I'm never one to back down from a challenge. "What are the rules?"

"Twenty-one questions. No right or wrong, just answers. We start with a toast, then we let the games begin."

"You're on."

The bartender pours the first round. We lift our glasses and clink the short stubby containers. He slams his liquor, sucks on the lime, and squints at the sour taste.

"Whew. That's a good one. Your turn."

I reach back to my college days and take the entire rim into my mouth, holding my head back, allowing the alcohol to trail down my throat. The only time I use my hand is to remove the empty vessel. I don't even bite the lime.

"Wow, impressive," he says.

"Thank you. No reason we can't have a little fun while being serious. So, who gets first question?"

"Ladies first, of course."

"Okay. What's your angle?"

"What do you mean?"

"You seem like you are trying to accomplish something. Obtain a goal."

"I am."

"What is it? If I may ask."

The look of deep thought on his face gives me the feeling it's a serious aspiration.

"I don't want to say. You may try to derail me." He smiles and takes his shot. "Okay, my turn. Why are you single?"

I expected a question about my work performance or how did I get so good at my job? Or maybe what are my objectives? But nothing so personal. "How do you know I'm single?" I counter.

"For starters, it's a Friday night and you're here in a bar with me. You haven't once picked up your phone to check for messages or missed calls, and your watch hasn't flashed anything either."

I feel a bit awkward he knows so much about me, but I come up with a deflection. "Why are you noticing these things? Are you like obsessed with me or something?"

"Maybe," he replies as he takes another shot.

"Well, why are *you* here then? Don't you have a girlfriend or friends at home waiting on you?" I try my damndest to sound tough, but his single-word answer has me shook a little. *What the fuck he means, maybe?*

"I don't have a girlfriend or friends, as you say. I had one, but she didn't keep me intrigued, and our lives were on a different course."

"Oh, I see. I'm sorry, I didn't mean to—"

"You didn't. I volunteered."

We both take another hit of tequila, and the in-house DJ changes the song to *Breathe* by Shania Twain.

"Oh, wow. I haven't heard this song in a while," I say, bobbing my head along to the tune.

"My turn," he says, bringing my attention back to him. "Would you like to dance?"

Okay, shit has become awkward as hell. He stands and takes my hand into his, and we move out to the designated dance area. Suddenly my senses are alive. I work with Lucas Weathers and have for the past two years. Never have I noticed his height puts him about six inches above me, even with my heels on. Or he smells like sweet sex on a king-sized bed with two thousand five hundred thread count sheets. Or his arms around my waist feel like they belong there. Our bodies swing natural, and I lose myself in his eyes.

"You okay?" he asks.

"Yeah, why wouldn't I be?"

"You haven't told me to fuck off or not to touch you."

He looks at me and grins, but I turn my head to break the small, but very real trance. Lucas Weathers, tall, dark-brown hair, with piercing gray eyes, an athletic build, and a sexy smile.

"Well, I can be nice at times." The song ends, and I make an excuse to leave the dance floor. "Thank you for the dance. It was nice. Even if it was with you."

I laugh, and he joins me as I walk back to the bar. We continue our conversation and game of questions until last call. The one bottle sustained us since we danced and even joined in the fun of the crowd when singing songs like *YMCA* or *Macarena*. He told me he loved the way my hips moved when I was doing the dance steps. I blushed at his comment, which rendered me speechless.

"Greene, are you driving home?"

"Call me Simone, and no, I sent for an Uber. I'm gonna go stand outside to catch some fresh air while I wait."

"Mind if I join you? Warning, I'm coming either way. I have to make sure no one messes with you."

I throw my hands up, giving into his request/demand. I grab my wristlet and offer to pay for half the bar tab. Shot down again.

He places his arm around my waist and steadily guides me outside where we wait for the driver.

"This was nice. Maybe we can do this again? But with dinner?" he says.

"Lucas Weathers, are you asking me out on a date?" I giggle through my question, not because it's funny, but we're rivals, and tonight, that disappeared.

"Maybe," he replies with a smile.

"If I said yes, how will we coordinate our outing?"

"Are you saying yes?" He looks at me with those damned eyes, and his bottom lip glistens in the glare of the streetlight.

"Maybe," I retort, using his single word against him. I go into my wristlet to get my house key out and drop the whole damn thing.

He bends to help me pick up the contents, and when we stand, you can't deny the electricity between us. It's been building all night, and I swear it's like a powder keg about to go off.

"Here's your pen," he says, breaking the tension.

Words fail me once again as I stand there, my breath catching and my mouth slightly ajar until I bite my bottom lip. I cast my gaze away from his stare, only for it to land on his fitted jeans and the semi-erection they're holding hostage. I glance back up, meeting his intent glare. My emotions are building within me, and I'm about to lose my composure.

"Fuck it," I say and I crash my mouth onto his.

Our tongues swirl and dip in and out of each other's mouths, neither wanting to concede to the other. The tips of his fingers gently press against the back of my head the deeper he dives into my mouth. I don't know where this attraction is stemming from—the alcohol, open conversation, natural stimulation—but I am enjoying every minute of it. The passion comes to an abrupt halt when the Uber driver arrives.

"Call for Simone?" he says when he pulls up beside the curb.

"Yeah, that's me," I acknowledge.

"I guess I'll see you at work on Monday," Lucas says, turning away and beginning to walk towards his car.

I don't reply. Instead, I grab his hand and pull him into the car with me, because I always close the deal.

CHAPTER FOUR

We go at it like two teenagers at a hilltop overlook. The driver attempts to make small talk, but I can only focus on Lucas' hand caressing my thigh as he moves it up my leg and under my skirt. His kisses land softly on my neck, and his tongue outlines my collarbone. Low moans and hisses escape my mouth before his covers mine again.

"Ma'am, we've arrived at your location," the driver interrupts.

We sit up, grabbing our composure and adjust our clothes before exiting the car. I clasp his hand as we walk up the short set of stairs to my front door. The entire time I have a mental discussion if I'm doing the right thing while my intoxication begins to wear off. We reach the door, and I punch in my access code and turn to Lucas to make sure he's aware of what's about to happen on the other side.

"Lucas," I say his name, and before I know it, he crashes his mouth into mine keeping me captive.

I drop my clutch while he reaches behind me and turns the knob, opening the entryway. The weight of our bodies thrusts us inside. His quick reaction braces us so we don't crash to the floor, but it doesn't stop us from knocking over my lamp and a few pictures when we bump into my table. I fumble around with the belt on his jeans, trying to unbuckle it while he slides my cardigan from my shoulders, allowing it to fall to the floor. I step out of my heels as we continue to undress each other, stumbling and bumbling around the furniture. He lifts and backs me into the wall, moving his lips down my neck to the top of my breasts. The passion in his kisses heightens my senses, and suddenly it's not the liquor driving me, it's *him*.

"Lucas," I moan while he unsnaps the garter and rolls my thigh-high stocking down, removing it, then repeats for the other side.

He slides his finger along the seat of my panties, and I know they're soaked with my excitement.

"Damn, you're wet," he mumbles in my ear. He suckles at my lobe while his fingers slip and slide inside my slickened lips.

I struggle to fight the intense pressure I'm feeling below, and a moan escapes my mouth, giving him clear indication of how much I'm enjoying this. "Lucas," I call out. Speaking the unspoken want within me.

He wastes no time taking me to the couch, sitting me

down, and kneeling; looking at my swollen lips longingly. He slips his fingers into the band of my undies and slides them off my body. Pulling me closer to the edge, he positions my feet on his shoulders and buries his face into my pussy, his skillful tongue diving in and out of my opening, making circles around my clit before he gently sucks. Each motion sends pulses down my legs and back up through my body.

Amidst my throaty moans and groans, I call out to him, "Lucas," in bated breaths. He continues, not giving me a break. My hips rise and feet curl when his tongue moves at a rapid-fire speed, bringing my heightened senses to an eruption point. "Shhhh..." I exhale, wanting to howl like a wolf baying at the moon when I explode.

He doesn't stop, and I ride the wave until my body stops convulsing.

"Fuck," I say when he finally separates his face from my pussy. An orgasm is the perfect nightcap for the week I've had, but the gaze from his eyes tell me it's not over.

Lucas stands there, stroking his dick and licking his lips then biting the bottom one. "Oh, that was just the appetizer, now I need my meal."

I stare helplessly at the size and girth of the monster before me. I swear it's like a third leg. *He's gonna fuck me sober with that thing*, I think to myself. After the verbal assault my pussy took, I can only imagine what she is going to endure now. But we love a challenge.

He leans down over me, taking my bottom lip between his teeth and gently bites and covers my mouth with his.

This shouldn't be happening, I think to myself. But I allow the ecstasy to overpower me. I turn to a more comfortable position, and he hovers above me, still kissing me and stroking his dick until I take over. I gently caress and tease his balls with one hand while the other moves in an up-and-down motion, digging my nail softly into the head.

Continuing my caressing action, he relaxes and takes a sitting position, tossing his head back in pleasure, and letting out a deep, throaty moan.

"Fuck, Simone. Don't stop. That shit feels so good," he says.

My pussy is getting jealous of all the attention she's not getting, especially when I squeeze out a good amount of precum. I know he's clean. We've had those tests done by one of our clients for free, and I snuck in and saw his results, looking for something on him. You know, for our office battles. Not that I even imagined doing this. Without a second, rather, third thought, I ease onto his cock and gently slide down, making my mini-girl happy. He locks eyes with me and grips my hips tightly. Guiding my hips in the same direction my hand took earlier. Getting a hang of the size of the beast, I speed up my actions, pumping him harder and faster. My walls are wetter with the tension building between my legs. I slow to a deep grind and rock my hips in circles.

His right hand grips tighter while his left grabs my hair and pulls my head back, exposing my neck. He buries his face in the crevice of my breasts and licks the sweat forming between them while he, too, thrusts in sync with my movement. He slides us off the couch and crouches with me still on top. He maneuvers my legs onto his shoulders and rests upon his knees.

This is a position I ain't ever been in, but I'm not complaining. The change up stimulates not only my clit but my G-spot as well. I'm not prepared for what my body is about to go through, I can tell.

He supports my back with his hands as he pushes deep, and I hold on for dear life.

"Tell me when you are coming," he mutters through clenched teeth.

The room seemingly spins, and my toes curl. "Lucas, I'm—"

With one final push, we both erupt simultaneously. My legs are a quivering mess as they rest on his shoulders, and I fall back.

He takes them down, not before kissing each of them. After a few minutes, silence falls around us, and I drift off to sleep.

There is nothing worse than cotton mouth after a night of drinking. I look at my phone, with surprisingly twenty-seven percent battery left, and see it's almost eleven AM. "Fuck," I say. Glancing around, I see that Lucas is still here, passed out on my floor next to me, *naked*. I run my hands over my face and through my hair, disgusted at what I succumbed to last night. Part of me was very aware and conscious, the other half flat-out didn't care. It was some dick, and we needed it. Now when all cylinders are firing, the afterthought of last night is *I fucked my rival*. I shudder when I think of that and want to get him out of here fast.

"Lucas," I call. He remains motionless. "Lucas," I raise my octave a little more, and it still doesn't garner a response.

Smack

I slap him a bit on his thigh, and he jumps up, hitting his head on the table.

"Fuck!" he exclaims while rubbing his boo-boo.

"Oh shit, I'm sorry. I had to make sure you were alive since I called you twice and there was no response. Didn't mean to startle you."

His gray eyes look at me with a hint of 'fuck off'. I think he sees through my façade. "What time is it anyway?" he asks as he presses the power button on his phone to turn it back on.

"Eleven o'clock," I reply. I gather all his things and hand them to him. "I'm sorry. I have to meet my mom in an hour, so..."

"Yeah, yeah. No worries. I have to pick up my dad

from the airport, then we are going to go grab a bite so he can tell me all about his trip."

He slides his jeans back on, sans underwear, and I can't help but watch him put the monster back inside. I shake the impure thought away and focus on the brush-off attempt at hand.

"Oh, sounds lovely. Look, can you lock the bottom on your way out? I'm gonna go hop in the shower. Thank you for a nice evening." I saunter off to my bedroom and secure the door so he can't follow. I take a few moments to listen intently for the front door to close. When it does, I scurry to my window and see him walking down the street to a waiting car. I take a deep breath and go start my shower.

As the temperature of the water warms, I look through my closet for something to wear. Seeing how my time is limited, I grab a pair of jeans with little rips, a classic rock t-shirt, and, of course, chucks. Setting my items on the bed, I get in the water and allow it to wash off the remnants of last night, or was it this morning? Either way, I want to rid myself of the experience. It wasn't a bad one. No, in fact, it was…fuck it. It was amazing.

My body felt charges it has never felt before. And those positions…I didn't know I was so limber. Didn't know he was so big. He is cocky, and arrogant, and…sexy as sin allows. But he's my rival. We're enemies when it comes to work. I shouldn't even be thinking about his piercing gray eyes or plush pink lips or… seemingly forked tongue. I bite my bottom lip when I think of how that one part of his body had me coming apart at the seams. Quickly, I let out a deep sigh and shake my head before *he* causes another orgasm, but at the mercy of my hands. I continue to bathe, putting all of yesterday's memories behind me and go meet my mom for lunch.

CHAPTER FIVE

When my mom's plane touched down, you would've thought I was a young kid all over again. See, my parents divorced five years ago, and at my urging, I suggested she go on this single for seniors' cruise. The stories she told me about the man she met had me quite intrigued. But she wanted to talk to me about starting a new relationship before she jumped into one. I thought it was sweet, seeing how I'm the only child. I think it's her way for me to low-key tell Daddy to see how he'll react.

"Mommy," I shout as I run to hug her when she enters the airport gate area.

"Aww, look at my baby. All grown up with her big financial job."

Nina Greene, fifty-five years young and currently single. Smooth and flawless mocha-brown skin like ribbons of chocolate. Hazel-brown eyes, with long salt-and-pepper hair that she never puts chemicals in. Wish I could say the same.

"Mom, I am so glad you are here. I miss you being around." We're originally from Michigan, but once I graduated from the blue and maize, I moved to Chicago to start my career. I thought Mommy would follow me after the divorce, but she has a paid-off house, car, and other things she obtained in the settlement.

"Well, I am here for a few weeks while Charles gets his business matters together."

"Oh, you're meeting him here?"

"Well, yes. Didn't you get my message, love?"

I recall the missed voicemail on my phone from her but I assumed it was a reminder of when to pick her up.

"To be honest, Mom, I didn't listen to it. I figured you were telling me the flight schedule. Anyway, let's go grab lunch. I'm starving."

"Sure. I want to try this Chicago Cut Steakhouse I've heard so much about. It's right on the river, and they say the views are spectacular."

"Great idea. We'll stop at my place and then go there for lunch. I'll make the reservation."

"Oh, no need. love. I already did when I got off the plane. I knew you couldn't say no to Mother.""

I signal for the skycap to help with her bags and I pop the trunk on my car, giving him a nice tip, and we go to drop off her luggage before heading to lunch.

On the way to my place, Mother casually mentioned I'll be meeting her beau at this luncheon. I figure it would be best for me to look a bit more presentable than casual, even though she said it would be okay. She also changed her ensemble to this full-bodied jumper with slits in the legs. Now I know my mother is in great shape and doesn't look like she's anywhere near her fifties, but this is too much leg for her to be showing.

"Uh, Mom. You're not going clubbing, and even if you were, that's still too much skin to be showing. Don't give him the wrong impression."

"Oh, my poor, green baby. He's seen me in my best suit, and I had no complaints," she says with a smirk as she walks to the bathroom to spray on her perfume.

My eyes roll at the thought of my mother having relations with any man.

"Mom, some things I don't need to know." I wave my hands and grab my lip gloss to apply.

Soon we are in the car heading to the Riverwalk for lunch.

We enter the swanky eatery off the Chicago river and follow our hostess to our awaiting guest. Along the way, Mom stops me for a moment.

"Now, Simone, I really like this guy, and he likes me, too. I don't want you to pass your judgy eyes or comments in his presence. Save them for later this evening, please."

My mom knows me well and knows how crass and blunt I can be, but I see this is important to her.

"I promise."

She takes my hands and gives them a gentle squeeze before we continue to the waiting guest.

"Ah, there she is. I was thinking you stood me up." A tall, gray-haired man with blue eyes, stands to greet my mother.

He gives her a kiss, and I smile when I see how happy she is.

"Now, you know I would never stand you up."

I feel like a third wheel but even more awkward as I call attention to myself.

"Ahem," I clear my throat, and they turn my direction.

"Oh, Charles, I'm sorry. This is my daughter Simone. Monie, this is Charles."

I think of how my mother never calls me Monie unless she's around family or someone real close. He must be the latter. "Hi, nice to meet you."

"You too, darling. My, you are just as beautiful as your mother."

"Thank you." I blush. This man is charming.

"Here, why don't you ladies take a seat, and I'll going to go see if my child has arrived." He pulls out two seats opposing each other for my mother and I to take. "Well, never mind, the eagle has landed."

"Dad, sorry I'm late. Work took a lot out of me yesterday."

The hairs on my neck stand when I hear that voice. *It can't be,* I think to myself. I close my eyes and say a silent prayer. *Oh please, please, please, don't let this be—*

"Nina, Monie, this is my son, Lucas. Son, this is Nina and her daughter, Simone."

Prayer unanswered. I stand to be polite and see the smirk he usually has dissipate at the same time our gaze meets.

"Ms. Nina, it's a pleasure meeting you," he says coyly before kissing the back of my mother's hand.

He does a great job concealing any emotions towards me, last night, or this shocking revelation. If I hadn't spent the last two years in an office battle with him, he'd fool me, too. But, the tension in his shoulders and the lack of eye contact tells me otherwise.

"You, too, Lucas. Your father has spoken well of you," my mother says once he takes the seat beside me.

"Monie, aren't you going to say something to the young man?"

I look to him, contemplating my answer, only to see a scowl on his face. My intuition screams resentment from him, leaving me to believe this morning left a bad taste in his mouth.

"No, Mother. I'm not," I say with vinegar on my lips.

"We already know each other. We're co-workers." I relax my breaths, trying not to let his demeanor affect me in front of our parents.

"Oh, what a small coincidence," Mr. Weathers says with a hearty laugh. "So, you must've been up late with work, too," he says.

"Well, Dad, I'm sure we don't want to discuss last night, *right*, Simone," Lucas interjects with his elbows rested on the table, still refusing to look at me.

I inhale deeply and straighten my shoulders. "I agree. Some things shouldn't be discussed or ever thought about again."

The waiter arrives, halting whatever snarky remark he'd surely follow up with. "I see your guests have arrived, Mr. Weathers. Can I get you all something to drink?"

"I'll have a Manhattan, and my love will have a mimosa."

"Very good, sir. And what can I get you two?"

"I'll have a scotch with a twist of lime," Lucas states.

"I'll have the same. Make it a double," I add.

"Must've been some project y'all worked on," Mom chimes in.

We say nothing, just give awkward glances at each other.

"Well, Lucas had a hot date, too, from what he told me. He left her place around eleven this morning. "

I choke on my water when Mr. Weathers begins to tell our business, not knowing I'm the girl Lucas was with.

"Oh, my. Well, Monie hasn't had any romantic interests in a while. I wonder if she's gonna end up alone."

I was waiting on the 'why is my daughter single' spiel. From the debutante scene, head cheerleader in both high school and college, and the sorority life, my parents figured I'd have a storybook life. But I never aspired to be the 'little woman' or even the equal half of anyone. I've always been career driven and goal orientated.

"Mother let's not talk about me. This is yours and Mr. Weather's moment to share. So, what are your plans?"

They take a loving look at each other and smile before answering.

"That's what we wanted to talk to you two about," Mother begins.

"When I met Nina on the cruise, I knew she was what I wanted in a friend and a companion."

"And I knew Charles was a man I wanted to spend more than seven days with. He's so chivalrous, and charming, and an excellent dancer."

"Don't forget kisser," he says pulling my mother's mouth to his.

"Dad, really? Right now?" Lucas sounds almost as angry as I feel.

"Son, what about the young lady you were with. You told me she was…"

"Dad, I'm not saying anything about the relationship, just the PDA," he quickly interjects.

This has me completely interested in what he mentioned to Pops. I look at him, and he casts his glance away from me.

"Well, we talked and talked some more, and—"

"Charles asked me to marry him."

My mouth drops open, and my eyes flutter a few times. "Ma-ma-marry?" I stutter.

"Yes, and we want y'all there to serve as our wedding party."

We both look at each other with surprise and concern.

"I was expecting a little more happiness from that side of the table," my mother not-so-subtly says to Mr. Weathers.

"Oh, I'm sorry. It took me, and I'm sure, Simone, by surprise, Mrs. Greene."

The server returns with our drinks, and I gulp mine and signal for another.

"Yeah, Mom. I'm totally fine. Just really, really, shocked. So, I assume you two have lots of things to plan and workout, so I'm guessing six months to a year before the ceremony."

"No, dear. We are getting married Friday afternoon."

Now it's Lucas' turn to have a spit-take. I shake my head as I keep my giggles to myself.

"Oh, I'm sorry. Don't you think it's a bit sudden?" Lucas asks the question we both want an answer to.

"No, son, I don't. I married your mother, God rest her soul, the same day we met. Two young and wild know-it-alls from Connecticut. We had you ten months later and were together until she passed three years ago. But there is no need for me to sit around and wallow in pity. I love Nina. We spent every day on the cruise together, learning about each other. Asking all the questions and sharing stories of our past and our kids. When we docked back in Florida, instead of saying I'll call you, I asked her to marry me. The thought of not being with her gave me the courage to take a chance."

The look they give each other is so tender and sweet. I can't be mad at their hasty decision. I didn't even know Lucas had lost his mother. Those memories are still in his gray eyes as I look at him staring at his dad.

I fumble around with my phone to try to get us away from the table. With this news, we need to talk about putting aside our differences. "Um, excuse me. Lucas, I got a message from Armstrong. Let's step over here and discuss a response. Would you two excuse us for a moment?"

We step aside to a hall right off the main floor near to the restrooms.

"What?" He comes at me, stern and uncaring. Not even in his usual joke-filled manner.

"Um, I want to say, for the sake of my mom and your dad, I'm not going to interfere with their happiness. It's clear they're taken with each other, and who am I to stop them. So, that's all."

"Okay," he says, flippant as he turns to walk away.

"Excuse me? '*Okay?*' That's all you have to say?"

"Yeah. What else do I need to say to the princess?"

I realize this is about our morning and I must smooth it over with him so the tension between us will cool down. "I'm sorry. I apologized to you this morning for pushing you out. But I had to meet with my mom."

"Yeah, I know. I wanted things to end differently."

I find myself growing frustrated with him. "How did you expect it to end? I mean, we bonded over drinks and a fuckfest before succumbing to sleep. That's all. Nothing else."

He grabs me into his arms, and kisses me with force while backing me into a wall. I want to—need to—fight it, but I can't. My body awakens with his actions, and I drape my arms around his neck.

"Please say you'll stop by tonight?" he whispers in my ear.

My breath fights to find its way back into my lungs. "I can't. I have my mom as a guest and now a wedding to plan."

He backs away, leaving me horny as fuck, and walks back to the table.

"Damn," I quietly say to myself. I run to the ladies' room and reapply my nude gloss and fix my hair before rejoining them at the table. When I get there, he's nursing a fresh drink and enjoying the conversation.

"Oh, there you are, dear. I was wondering if you had to run to the office. Lucas said you seemed a bit distracted," my mom says.

"Huh? Oh, yes. Trying to work out a new situation." I disguise my sexual frustration with a flimsy excuse.

"Hey, sis, I took the liberty of ordering you another drink," Lucas slyly comments while passing my drink to me.

"That's right, you two will finally have a sibling. Lucas always wanted a sister he could protect, and now he'll have you."

The parentals laugh, but little do they know, Lucas has already *had* me.

"Shall we order?" I say, turning the heat off me.

"Yes, let's do. I am famished. My plane ride was long due to the layover. Which reminds me, Monie, your aunts, Gwen and Beverly, will be here Wednesday. They can take the guest room and I'll bunk with you. They're going to help plan the reception."

"Oh, I have a great place that we can host the event. This guy I know has this little hall he rents out. I'm sure he'll have it available for me," Mr. Weathers offers.

"Nonsense, Simone has a lovely place with a nice rooftop. We can have it there. And her aunts have a restaurant back home so they can put the menu together."

"I have a friend who can get us liquor at cost since I

manage their financial account and saved them a ton of money last quarter," Lucas chimes in.

"I didn't hear Simone agree," Mr. Weathers says.

I'm about to answer when Lucas' hand runs slowly up my thigh under my belted shirt dress, casually, without bringing attention to us. I become flustered, and my answer comes out a bit awkward.

"I'd *love* to host the, uh, celebration," I squeal.

His hand continues up to the waistband of my thong, where he pulls and snaps the fabric before removing his fingers.

"Mom, Lucas and I have some reports to go over tonight, and I may be over at his place late. Oh, wait, Mr. Weathers will be there. We shouldn't bore him with all the fussing about reports and stuff."

"Oh, he's used to it. I did it for his company for four years." Lucas does not help me devise a plan to have another night with him.

"Well, I guess we can work on the report over the phone," I say, conceding defeat.

"I'm sure we can get an extension and wait until Monday when we get more details."

"True," I say, running out of clever covers for our secret rendezvous.

Our parents are engaged in a moment of their own, looking at and discussing pictures from their trip. Stirring my beverage to mix the ingredients, I struggle to find ways to talk.

"Excuse me," I say as I stand from the table.

Lucas and his dad, being the chivalrous kind, rise as well.

"Is everything all right, dear?" my mother asks.

"Yes, ma'am. I need to go make a phone call to my assistant. I'll be right back." My gaze rests upon Lucas' facial expression, and I see a damn smirk forming. Like he knows he has me rattled and is enjoying it. I continue to step outside to gather a much-needed breath of fresh air.

I smile at the passersby when I find a seating area outside the establishment. I close my eyes and try to wrap my head around the events over the past twenty-four hours. How did we go from arch enemies to fuck buddies? And why have I never noticed his tattoos? Or the fact he is an only child like me? And why am I so turned on by him? My phone rings, and I answer it very casual and informative.

"Yeah," I say.

"Why did you run off? Were you thinking about me?" His voice melts the airwaves and penetrates through my icy demeanor.

"Lucas, what do you want?"

"Room nine-two-eight. Eight o'clock tonight."

The phone conversation ends, and I realize he didn't tell me where, only a room number. My phone buzzes, taking me by surprise, and I see it's a message from my mom.

Mom: *Your food is getting cold, dear.*

I eagerly rejoin them at the table and jump in on the conversation.

"Sorry about that. What did I miss?"

"Oh, Lucas was telling us the next project would be working with some big shot and they wanted to set up a meeting at the Langham. I figure they must be quite posh to want a meeting at such a lavish hotel," his dad says.

Now I know where to meet him.

CHAPTER SIX

7:59, 7:59, 7—8 *o'clock.*
I take a deep breath and knock on the door of room nine-two-eight. It opens, and standing before me is a man I never thought I would fuck even once, but now we look to be heading to the second-time zone. I went home, showered, shaved and waxed, and put on a little bare midriff top and jeans with a pair of heels. Mom thinks I'm going out with my friends, Hailey and Natalie, but they are both out of town for a week. I did tell her I may be home late. She had her iPad and was Facetiming her fiancé when I left. I don't even want to think of what they may or may not be doing.

"Hi." I push the word out of my mouth as if it's my first.

He doesn't respond. Instead, he takes my hand and places a sweet kiss on the back of it.

"You look amazing, as always."

"You've only seen me in my work clothes, except for today's lunch."

"Like I said, amazing as always."

I blush at his comment and forget we are sworn enemies. He guides me to the couch in this one-bedroom suite and takes off my heels.

"I have some fresh strawberries and wine or champagne if you prefer."

I haven't eaten since lunch, and I made sure to drink plenty of water and take an aspirin to stave off any hangover.

"I'll take a glass of wine and a few strawberries," I request.

He goes to the wet bar and retrieves the items before returning to the sofa. He pours two glasses and hands me one of them. "Here you go, Monie." He chuckles.

"Oh my gosh. Don't start." I laugh in retort because there is nothing worse than your rival having not one, but two, things on you and you have nothing. "So, why'd you pick this hotel? I mean, I'm sure there was somewhere else we could've met up." I look around the room at the features and embellishments. I don't have to guess about the price tag since I already know. One of the sorority mixers was held here, and a few of us inquired to the cost of the room for the weekend so we could split the bill.

"I have a friend who is a manager here, and he owed me a favor."

"Nice connection to have."

"We went to college together, so it's a little more than a connection."

I nod and find myself nervously tapping my glass. I don't know what, if any, conversation we should be having. I mean, do I say something or wait on him? What subject do we talk about? I decide to freestyle it. Whatever comes out is the answer.

"So, is this the cheesy part of the evening where you put on music to seduce me?" I ask, trying to ease into my anxiety.

"No." He laughs. "I don't need to seduce you. I've already captivated you."

I don't deny or fight the fact he's right. I am so very much his capture. "Oh, so what do we do now?"

He takes the glass from my hand and sets in on the table before picking me up and cradling me in his arms. We ease our way to the bedroom where he lays me on the bed.

I start to remove my clothes, but he stops me.

"No. I'll do that. Give me a few moments." He scurries back to the living room area and turns out all the lights, coming back with the bowl of strawberries and chocolate syrup, placing them on the nightstand. He takes off his shirt with one move, revealing the tapestry of art adorning his physique.

I let out a slow breath at the sight before clearing my

throat. "I never knew you had so many tattoos. They're really nice."

"Yeah, it's sort of cathartic for me. Started off as a rite of passage when I turned eighteen and it grew from there. Each thing that bought me pleasure or pain was memorialized."

"Can I get a closer look?" I ask.

He sits next to me, and I go over each tattoo. From religious symbols to the portrait of his mother over his heart. He also has a symbol representing his zodiac sign, and a few sexy ones of busty women.

"Are any of these women former girlfriends or lovers?" I snidely inquire.

"No, only the ones they have at the ink shops."

I run my hands over each marking, getting a bit aroused. Something about a man with ink drives me crazy. I didn't get much time to marvel at his collection last night, seeing as I was in an alcohol-induced cloud.

I think he catches on to my stimulation and runs his thumb across my bottom lip. I, in turn, bite it and feel his heart beat skip. He takes a strawberry and replaces his thumb with the fruit. The sweetness spills down my chin when my teeth tears into its flesh. But he's there to lick every drop.

He hands me the bowl and holds my feet into his hands where he massages them, maneuvering in circular motions from the heel up to my toes. As he kneads my body, I relax. He reaches into the nightstand and takes out massage oil, pours some into his palms, and works it into my skin. I close my eyes, forgetting that no more than thirty-six hours ago, I couldn't stand to be near him, but now I can't bear to be away from him. He kneads the flesh of my tootsies, gently, seductively, semi-erotically. The more I relax, the more I feel parts of me tingle that shouldn't happen from a foot massage.

"Mm." A moan escapes me, giving him a hint of how much I'm enjoying his touch.

He pauses for a minute to unbutton my pants and remove them. I don't fight. In fact, I lift my hips to aid in my de-pantsing. He pulls me to an erect position and removes my crop top, leaving me in nothing but my La Perla lingerie.

"Would you have a problem if I took your hair down from your ponytail?" He twirls it around his fingers, taking a handful into his grasp and gently pulling my head back where he places gentle bites along my neckline.

"No, go ahead," I reply.

He carefully removes my hair cuff, allowing my tresses to fall into an unruly pattern. He massages my scalp, starting off with light and tender strokes before increasing the pressure. He moves down to the base of my neck and uses slow, circular motions against my skin, pressing into my flesh.

"Ah," I say as the increase of pleasure reaches my clit.

"Did I hurt you?"

"No, the opposite. This feels amazing. Almost—"

"Climatic?"

"Yesss," I breathe out.

He expands his fingers down my shoulders and over to my spine where he plays it like a fine-tuned piano. I lie down, face-first, giving him full access to my entire back. Calmly and sensually the motions continue, engaging me in a deep relaxation and peaks of near orgasm.

He turns me over and relaxes beside me, propped up on his elbow, lusciously tracing the outline of my body with the tips of his fingers.

"Did you enjoy the massage?" he inquires with a sinful smile.

I can't think of anything to say. I'm enthralled by his gaze, and it beckons me, commands me, calls me. I push him onto his back, straddling him before taking his mouth with mine. Not a rushed kiss, but a slow, lingering, tongue-dancing, I-could-do-this-all-night mouth journey. I reach down and undo his jeans and find he is without underwear.

"Do you like going commando?" I ask, easing the denim over his hips.

"Yeah, when I'm at home. I like to have one less thing to get in my way of relaxing." He lifts his pelvis to assist with the removal.

I stroke him from base to shaft to head and back down again, feeling him harden with each pass. The way his veins pulsate and his breath hitches makes me crave him even more. Removing my thong bikini, I ease myself onto his cock, gradually rocking my hips back and forth.

"Simone," he calls out, dragging the 's' in my name while gripping my hips. "Damn, baby, you do that so good," he adds.

In my mind, I make a checklist to come back to the 'babe' comment. I'm sure it's the heat of the moment. I change up my motion and move more in a circular pattern. This proves to be the thing he loves. He tilts his head back, and I lean in to lick his prominent Adam's apple. I switch to using up-and-down actions, and he grips me even tighter holding my gaze with his.

There are no words spoken, not even the sounds you would hear between a couple enthralled in passion. We look at each other as I maintain the lead position.

"You're going to make me come if you keep doing me like you do," he says, breaking the silence.

"Isn't that the goal? To make you come?" I softly speak into his ear, biting his lobe in the process.

He pulls me closer and takes my breasts into his mouth, sucking my nipples to an erect point then lavishly licking on them, intensifying my growing senses. I let out a moan, and my rhythm increases speed. The sweat between us slicks my already wet pussy as we continue to slam into each other.

"Wait, wait," he says, stopping all movement.

"Something wrong?" I manage to get out with half breaths.

"No, nothing's wrong. You were on top last time, it's my turn."

He grins and quickly flips our position, my back meeting the coolness of the sheets. He laps at the sweat covering my belly and up to the divide between my mountains before sliding his massive dick back into me, and my senses pick up right where they left off.

On instinct, I wrap my legs around his waist, tilting my hips up with each thrust and bracing for the ensuing ride.

"Lucas, I can't hold back much longer," I say when the excitement below builds, signaling a forthcoming ending to a long and steamy session.

"Come for me, baby. Let it go," he growls through his deepening thrusts. "Fuck, Simone," he calls out to the passion unleashing within and collapses on top of me.

I follow his lead, digging my heels into his hips and my nails in his back. "Lucas, Lucas, Lucas," I moan, my legs falling like jelly from their perch.

We lie there gulping for air, soundly like we both finished running a marathon. He slowly rolls to his back, draping his hand across his forehead. I prop up on my elbow and look at the beautiful man lying next to me. It's my turn to trace and trail fingers to places unexplored. I start with his abs, and he clenches, letting out a slight giggle.

"Babe, stop. I'm ticklish," he explains.

There's that word again. I figure with all the fun out

the way, now's a good time to discuss. "Why do you keep calling me babe or baby?" I ask. I go over his nipples, and they contract at my touch. My gaze drifts south, and I see they are not the only things responding.

He inhales deeply and releases before answering. "I was hoping you wouldn't mind, but I'm sensing this is only a fuck thing to you." Things down south go soft, and his body stops responding to my touch.

"It's not that I mind, I'm curious. We've been at each other for two years, and now I'm babe? Seems weird, that's all."

He turns over and catches my attention. "Hey, this is going to sound crazy, but I've had a crush on you since the day we met. I only kept up the mean-spirited rivalry so I could have interactions with you. I even remember what you wore the first time I saw you. You had on these gray pants that were made for your body and a white silky-like sleeveless top. I only knew it was sleeveless 'cause when we all went to lunch, you removed the matching jacket. I kept watching you like a man obsessed. I knew I wanted you and was determined to get you."

"Why didn't you go for it early on?"

"Well, you were pissed when Armstrong gave me that one athlete's account, and I think you've hated me ever since then."

I think back to how I busted my ass for that account and knew I had it when Jarron Brown, pro basketball all-star rookie of twenty-fourteen, sent me and Tanya flowers plus a gift basket of spa goods. Then Armstrong called a meeting and announced Lucas was the account manager. This was a guy I had good office rapport with, was new to the company, and he snagged the one thing I wanted so I could attract more clients like him. It's hard for women, especially African-American women, to be taken seriously in this field. So, he's right. I had it in for him ever since.

"Yeah, but I shouldn't have taken it out on you. I'm sorry."

"That's okay. You missed out on two years," he coyly states.

"Two years of what?" I laugh.

"This." He tilts my head towards him and kisses me. "And this," he says, moving his lips down to my neck, pushing me over on to my back. "And this." He eases his dick into my swollen, slick pussy, and my back arches when I brace for maximum insertion.

I relax, and he strokes softly, slowly, sweetly until we crash...two hours later.

CHAPTER SEVEN

I slept for most of Sunday. Hell, I didn't even get in until nine AM. Needless to say, my mother was pissed. Not that she was worried, but I didn't call. Lesson learned: you're never too old to not call your parents. The fact I even made it home should be commended. Lucas wanted me to stay and spend the entire day with him, and by my second orgasm of the early morning, he nearly had me convinced. Mother's text made the final decision. After a short nap, I took her to go find a nice dress to wear for her nuptials this Friday, then we had lunch before going back home where I slept until today. I didn't even bother to answer my messages from Lucas. His dad actually called my mom and asked if I was feeling okay 'cause Lucas wouldn't get out of bed. He thought maybe it was the food from brunch or something going around at work.

    I arrive at the office with a different walk than usual.

Not the I-spent-my-weekend-getting-my-back-broke-like-records walk, but a new outlook on life type of vibe.

"Good morning," I say to everyone I pass.

"You sure have a lively step this morning, Ms. Greene," the lobby receptionist says.

"Oh, yes. My mom is in town, and I love when she's here."

"Oh, really. I thought it had to do with those deep-purple hickeys on your neck."

The sudden stripe of horror hits me, and I fast pace to the elevator so I can get to my office and see what I missed. I was careful to put ice on them this morning after my shower and use my water-based concealer to hide the evidence.

"Ms. Greene, Mr. Armstrong—" Tanya begins to speak as I approach her desk.

"Not now, Tanya. I need to get something done really quick." I flash by her and run into my office, closing and locking the door. I shut the blinds and look at my neck. To help aid in my disguise, I wear a semi-high collared, sleeveless, thin sweater to help hide the passion mark from this weekend. Seeing how this isn't helping, I switch to a button-down blue shirt and use a silk scarf to help hide the evidence. I take out the emergency concealer usually reserved for surprise presentations after I've been up all night binging on TV and begin applying. This solidifies my point that having extra wardrobe in your office is a must. A knock at my door gives me even more reason to panic.

"Yes?" I calmly call out.

"It's Armstrong. Why is your door locked? Are you okay?"

I don't have time to do much blending, so I hurry and find my little nautical scarf I use on my hair and fashion a simple accessory before opening the door.

"Yes, Mr. Armstrong?"

He raises one eyebrow as he looks at me. "Going sailing later?" he quizzically and comically implies.

I do a little nervous giggle and offer up a phony excuse. "Oh, this? Pssh, I spilt um, coffee on my shirt and tried to clean it but made it worse. I had to change shirts, which is why the door was closed. Did you need me for something?"

"Uhhh, no. I am calling for a meeting of all heads today after lunch. A few changes are coming you may be interested in. Be in the big conference room sharply at one-fifteen PM."

I spot Lucas walking in, and he flashes me a smile before heading on to his office. I swear he's moving in slow motion and this is that fantasy sequence you see in movies.

"You hear me, Greene?" Mr. Armstrong's deep voice calls to me for understanding.

"Mmhmm, yes, sir. We'll be there."

He turns and walks away, and I nearly melt through

my shirt. I turn on my desk fan to the highest setting and lean in front of it, trying to will away the perspiration.

"Okay, what the hell is going on, Simone? You are never like this," Tanya asks when she steps into my office.

"I had a little early morning mishap with my coffee. You know, typical Monday."

"Nah, this is something else. You had a date this weekend, didn't you?"

How thin is my veil if she can see right through it? But of course, I'm gonna deny everything.

"No. I wouldn't have had time. I picked my mom up Saturday, met her new man, and then suddenly I'm planning a party on my rooftop for a wedding and reception. I just have a lot going on."

"Yeah. That must be it. You are completely frazzled. Anyway, the new reports are in for mailing, but I ran out of brochures."

"Oh, well, I will go down to the storage closet and grab a new box. Anything else we need?"

"Well, notebooks, pens, markers... Do you want me to go with?"

"No, I got it. I need to walk off my nerves anyway. Can you pull the team together for a meeting after Armstrong's? May as well get ready for the change."

"Maybe he's announcing that senior manager position today. That's what the rumor mill is buzzing about."

"I guess we'll find out at one-fifteen. I'll be back in a few." I head to our main storage located on the lower level of the building. I and the other account managers are the only ones who have access to this room. I exit the elevators and pull out my key card to gain entrance. I fumble around for the light switch, and when I do find it, only one fluorescent bulb comes to life, barely casting enough of a glow for me to see.

"Great," I mumble. Good thing I know where the cart and the items I'm looking for are located. I grab the shipping cart and walk towards the back of the seventeen by seventeen space where the boxed items are kept. I use the step stool to reach the sealed packs of brochures and folders and carry them back down to the waiting transporter.

"Hey, Monie," Lucas says.

His surprise appearance scares the shit out of me, and all the items in my hands fall from my grasp. "Fuck. Can't you make your presence known when you enter a room?" I yell.

"I'm sorry, the view was a sight to see for a Monday morning."

Okay, he wins with that corny line. "Still, you could've given me a heart attack." I reach out and hit him on his chest.

"So, what's the deal with the sailor's scarf?" he asks.

"It would appear someone left a hickey on my neck the size of a globe grape."

"Well, in his defense, I think he was getting some sweet pussy and was sucking on your neck to see if all of you was just as sweet." He nuzzles under my neck and feels under my skirt till he reaches my panties. Running his finger along the seat of them, he lets out a slow hiss when he feels the moisture already seeping through. "Is this for me?" he asks, nibbling on my ear.

"Yes," I breathe out.

He presses me against the wall, wrapping my legs around his waist and hiking my skirt up, exposing my cheeks since I'm wearing my undies of choice. "Why didn't you reply to my messages?" he asks, his fingers invading my sticky opening. He captures my lips with his, and his tongue forces its way in.

"I was resting since you wore my ass out," I reply.

He unbuckles his pants, lets them fall around his ankles, and pulls out the mini-monster, stroking it and slapping it up against my ass. I can feel his excitement seeping out as he moves his dick around.

"You still should've texted me." He slams into me deep and hard.

My still sore lips take the brunt of his thrust, and I yelp slightly.

"Ah, fuck."

He covers my mouth with his hand and continues to drive. We bump into the wall, and with each thrust I fear someone will hear us or something will fall from the top shelf. I dig my nails into his shoulders, gripping tightly when my orgasm comes out of left field.

"Fuck. Lucas, I'm coming."

He moves his hand from my mouth and presses my neck gently and shudder against his body. His grip tightens when he reaches his own peak. The veins in his neck pop, and he grits through the final thrusts. He leans his head on my chest while our breathing calms down.

"Have dinner with me?" he requests.

"Okay. Where do you want to go?"

"My place. I'll text you the address and time. I think our parents are going on a date tonight."

"Are you cooking, or do I need to bring something?"

He lets me back down, and I remove my undies, rendering them useless. Taking off his t-shirt, he uses it as a rag to clean himself up.

"I'll take care of everything. Be sure to bring a change of clothes. We can ride to work together tomorrow."

"I will bring myself and an overnight bag. What about your dad?"

"He's going to my uncle's later to help with some business things. So, we will have the place all to ourselves." He lands another kiss on my lips.

An unorthodox solution presents itself as I look around and spot some paper towels. Thankfully, I have personal wipes and a backup pair of panties in my office. "I look forward to it." I gather the rest of my items and straighten myself out before heading back upstairs.

Only the leads and their assistants could participate in the surprise meeting. We are all gathered around the table, and wouldn't you know, Lucas is sitting dead in front of me. As Armstrong goes on about how Kyle Bloomfield, a senior account manager, will be leaving at the end of the month, Lucas and I are exchanging texts.

Lucas: *I dropped my pen. I may need to go under the table to get it. Wonder what I will see while down there.*

Simone: *I wish you could taste what you'll see.*

He casually bends down to get his property and grazes my leg with his hand before returning to his seat.

"Everything all right, Weathers?" Armstrong asks.

"Uh, yes, sir. I dropped my writing equipment, and it rolled over by Ms. Greene's feet. I was trying not to get kicked."

Armstrong gives him an awkward eye, and the whole room looks towards me when I don't respond.

"Oh, I didn't have a clue what he was doing. I was listening intently to your presentation."

A few heads nod in agreement, and Armstrong continues.

Simone: *You're going to get us caught.*

Lucas: *I like the thrill of it all. BTW, where did those panties come from?*

Simone: *I keep a spare for unplanned incidents.*

Lucas: *Oh, I see. Don't have those on tonight.*

Simone: *And you don't wear anything over this.*

I remove my shoe, extend my leg, move my foot up his

leg, and nestle it against his junk. My gentle strokes awaken the beast underneath those slacks, and he squirms a little to adjust himself. He glances up at me and flashes a subtle smile. Meanwhile, I look towards Mr. Armstrong.

"So, that's why I am naming Lucas Weathers as our new senior account manager," he announces.

The room erupts in claps and whistles while my heart sinks. I turn back to Lucas, and he has a look of surprise on his face, but mine quickly turns to anger. I move my foot from his lap, and he stands to go shake Mr. Armstrong's hand. I fake a clap, but as I stare at him, I hope I'm boring a hole into his head.

"Lucas will be over the account teams led by Dominic and Simone. I trust you two won't have an issue with this." Armstrong studies us for agreement.

"No, sir. Lucas is a great guy, and I'm sure I will learn under his tutelage," Dominic Bright boasts.

What a kiss-ass, I think to myself. I continue to glare at Lucas who can't seem to make eye contact with me.

"Ms. Greene, do you have a problem?"

The heat from the others pours over me, and I cringe when I think he is my new lead. Kyle had been out of the office a lot recently, but he kind of put me in charge. The natural flow of things between Armstrong and myself seemed like I was a shoo-in to take his place. But once again, this asshole shows up and takes what should've been mine.

"No, sir," I simply state. No long, drawn-out, kissing

ass from me. In fact, Lucas won't be getting any more of this ass.

"Alrighty then. If you all don't have any other things to comment or bring to the table, we are dismissed."

Everyone stands to leave, and Tanya hangs around waiting for me to gather my things and put my shoe back on. I make a mental note to burn these stockings and everything he touched when I get home.

"Uh, Tanya, Simone will see you in a moment. I need to speak with her and Lucas. Please close the door on your way out," Armstrong says.

"Yes, sir. Simone, will we still be meeting?" she asks.

"I don't think so. Let's table it for tomorrow."

"Okay. See you in a few." She leaves to head back to our area.

I turn my attention to see why I am being held against my wishes.

"Simone, I want and need to know you will be okay working under Lucas. I know how much you wanted this position, but after I spoke with a few people and thought long and hard about the responsibilities and the client base he will oversee from both teams, he was the better choice. This has nothing, and I do mean nothing, to do with your performance at all. Most of the clients Dominic handles are male-based companies. Unfortunately, they are established companies, if you will, and not very open-minded."

Armstrong does his best to soften the blow, but the more he speaks and the more I think about it, I was flat-out played by Lucas. He knew he was going to get this position so he thought if he plied me with alcohol, ate me like a buffet, and fucked me three ways to New Years, I wouldn't be upset. I should've known.

"I will continue, business as usual." My glare never changes, and I can tell Lucas is rather uncomfortable, which is a little satisfaction.

"Good. Want to make sure there are no hard feelings. I need to talk with Lucas about the changes, so you can leave now."

I excuse myself and head to my desk. I can feel eyes leering at me while I walk by. I know the office gossip will be full of me flipping out in the meeting or getting passed over because I blew it with Clemet. Anything to start the office buzzing. I enter my office and place my head on the mahogany desk.

"You okay, boss?" Tanya asks, entering.

I raise my head, and she sees the streaks of tears on my face.

"Oh, honey. I'm so sorry." She rushes to my side to comfort me.

"I'm okay. I really wanted that position." I don't offer any more details.

A knock on the door halts our conversation, and I clean my face while she goes to answer it.

"I need to speak to Ms. Greene," Lucas demands as the door opens.

I sit up at attention when Tanya steps aside.

"Alone, Tanya," he says, not taking his eyes off me.

Tanya leaves, closing the door behind her.

"Yes, boss. How can I help you, boss?" I snidely say.

"Stop. You don't have to act this way, Simone."

"Well, how would you feel if you let your guard down for one minute, because maybe the asshole isn't one after all, then he stabs you in the back?" My voice increases, and I know people can hear me now. At this point, I don't care.

"You heard Armstrong say this wasn't an easy choice. I had no clue I was even being considered."

"Bullshit, Lucas. You knew since last week when we fought about the Clemet account you were going to get this position. Fucking me was just a prize. Or maybe you thought it would make the blow softer."

"Simone—"

"Get out. And unless it is work related, don't ever speak to me again."

"Our parents are getting married, remember. So I will be talking to you for the rest of our lives." He storms off, my door hitting the stop hard when he exits.

I can't believe all this shit is going on. Since Friday my life has been one roller coaster after another. One thing is for certain, I can't let my mom marry his dad.

CHAPTER EIGHT

My plans to thwart my mother's pending nuptials failed as soon as I hit my door on Tuesday evening. Mr. Weathers was over, and he bought my mom a diamond bracelet. Then they began to cuddle and coo on my couch. I greeted them with 'hello' and went straight to my room. It's obvious his son shares his relentless behavior when it comes to affection. Difference is, they're in a relationship, and we're not. I've been dodging his calls and messages, both text and video, since Monday. I use Tanya as my mouthpiece at work, and thankfully no one is any the wiser as to what is really going on.

"Simone, can we have a meeting about the acquisitions from last month? I need a full reconciliation of activity," Lucas says as he casually enters my office.

"Sure thing," I reply without even looking up at him.

He leans over my computer monitor, forcing his way into my visual. I give him the 'fuck off' glare, but he insists.

"Why are you ignoring me?"

"I'll have those reports to you in about five minutes since I'm already working on them. I also have my lead sheet for this month if you want to go over that as well." I don't break for his tactics, although those gray eyes try to start a mini fire down below, but I quickly extinguish that shit.

"Very well. I trust I'll see you at Thursday's pre-wedding dinner," he says on his way out the door.

I take a few moments to breathe in deeply and release a few times. In doing so, I catch the faint smell of his cologne. I never paid attention to the warm and inviting scent that is the perfect blend of spice and floral for man. It was all on me by Sunday morning and forgotten by Monday afternoon. I shake my head and continue with my work. A meeting maker pops up on my screen, and I accept it as a good employee should. I go to the cafeteria to grab a water since I left my tumbler at home this morning.

"Hey, Greene. Thanks for the assist yesterday with the Clemet account. I see why you're the best at what you do. I would've never picked up on that stock change like you demonstrated." Paul Edwards, the guy we both lost the account to last Friday, corners me into a conversation.

As we converse, I laugh and smile for the first time in a few days. I couldn't even binge-watch my favorite comedy last night to get me out of my mood. Lucas walks in, talking on the phone, and I can't help but wonder who has his attention. His smile is bright, and his eyes sparkle. He strolls past us, and I can hear the faint sound of a woman's voice on the opposite end.

"So, Paul, are you single? I don't recall seeing you with anyone at any of the parties. Oh, I hope I'm not prying. I thought we were having a nice conversation."

"Oh, no problem. I'm not seeing anyone currently. My ex and I recently ended our relationship about a month ago. After three years."

"I had no idea." I extend my hand to cover his, only in a show of support, letting my grasp linger a little longer than I should. I know this is petty, but I had to. Hearing *him* on the phone with whoever that was, upset me in a way.

"So, this is why you are not upstairs in my office, Ms. Greene?" Lucas snaps when he sees the physical contact between Edwards and me.

Holding back my urge to smile, I wasn't sure if my attempt would warrant any kind of reaction, but by his tone, I see it has. "Mr. Weathers, our meeting isn't for another fifteen minutes. I have my phone set to remind me."

"No, that's a team huddle. Had you opened the notification, you would've seen we were to talk immediately. But I'll take that matter up with you afterwards."

He storms out, and I'm left embarrassed and pissed. I chase after and catch him at the elevator as the doors are closing. I don't pay attention to the fact we're alone, but at this point I don't care.

"How the fuck is you going to talk to me like you did in front of my colleague? What were you trying to prove? You steal the job away from me and then flaunt your balls in front of the world."

"You walk around with this fucking chip on your shoulder covered in frost and don't open emails which contain important information because you think I stole your job. Well, take a look in the mirror, Simone. You cost yourself the job because of your hatred for me. I've done nothing but try to be nice to you, but if the princess doesn't get what she wants, the whole world be damned. Be in the conference room in five minutes."

The doors opened while he was letting me have it, so when he exits, the entire staff is looking our direction. I take the walk of shame to my office and hit print on the reports and get ready for the scheduled gathering.

"Simone, what was that about?" Tanya asks, sticking her head through the entrance.

"Did Armstrong hear it?"

"No, thankfully. He left for a meeting uptown. But everyone else heard how Lucas lit into you for not being in his office. Where did you go?"

"I misread the notification and was in the cafeteria."

"I see how you can lose track of time. But he was really livid."

"I heard him on the phone with some woman. He may

have been projecting onto me. Who knows." I fabricate a cover-up, not wanting to put our personal business out in the office. "I'll see you after the meeting," I say to Tanya. Taking the reports, I saunter to the conference room where Dominic and Lucas are chatting.

"Hey, Simone. Here, take my seat," Dominic offers.

"Thanks, Dom, but I think I'll hang out right here. You go ahead."

Lucas looks at me and rolls his eyes as I sit in my chair. A few others join, and Lucas begins. On the surface, I may look like I'm paying attention while he goes over closing out some of the things left open before Kyle moved on, I'm fuming.

He gives out assignments to each of us to help with the process. Even though I'm present, my mind is drifting back to the reaming I got near the elevator. That last part really hit me. The whole 'princess' thing.

"If no one has anything to add, you may all go back to your office. Have those accounts transferred and or closed by month's or their cycle end. Whichever is first."

We're dismissed and we all head to our respective places. Lucas whizzes past me with not so much as an 'excuse me' or 'move, bitch'. Glancing at the contents in my hand, I see the reports he requested. I make a U-turn and march into his office where his head is lowered while he reviews documents.

"Excuse me, Mr. Weathers," I shyly state.

He looks up to see it's me before returning to his work at hand. "What do you want, Greene?"

I'm thrown by his sudden change. This has only happened once, and that was Saturday at lunch with our folks. *What kind of chameleon am I dealing with?* "Mr. Weathers, here are those reports you asked about."

"Yeah, an hour ago, but better late than never, right?"

I go to speak, but a message from my mom interrupts, prompting me to request tomorrow off to help with last-minute things. "I also will not be in tomorrow. Leah will run point with the Bristol group and call me if needed, but all that information is in the email I cc'd you on earlier."

He doesn't speak, only continues to jot down information and mark through my report.

I find myself getting a little angry with his nonchalant attitude. "Did you hear me?" I ask.

"Yes, I heard you. But it seems you didn't hear me. Because in your world nothing matters if it's not what you want."

My heart gets this weird pain when those words are hurled at me. Not the nine-one-one type of pain, but a sharp truth about me. My eyes want to let loose the emotion hiding behind them, but I instead turn and step lively to my office. There are five people I find myself in need of at this moment. My mom, Aunt Beverly, Aunt Gwen, and Ben and Jerry.

"Tanya. I am done for the week, but I will have my

work laptop if I'm needed. My aunts are here, and I think I'll go join them for spa day."

"My, sounds great. I'll make sure Leah has the documents on PowerPoint for the meeting. Do I need to let Weathers know?"

I glance toward Lucas' office and see him standing at Mandy Gere's desk tee-hee-ing about something. She reaches out and touches his arm, her hand lingering, while laughing and flipping her blonde tresses. He catches me looking and steps away from Mandy towards our direction.

"No, I told Weathers, and I'm sure he'll tell Armstrong. I have a big thing with my mom Friday, so Armstrong expected me to be off, but I was going to try to get in my monthly with the client. Anyway, I'm out. See you Monday."

I walk to the elevator and press the button. Lucas slides beside me, but we say nothing at first. The doors open, and we both step in. I press the button for the garage, he presses for the main lobby.

"Did you get the food list for the reception?" he asks.

"Yes. I printed it and placed it in my princess folder," I snap back.

"Well, my dad is pretty particular about those cupcakes."

"I already placed the order Tuesday when I was ignoring you. I want to make sure my stepdad is happy with his..."

"No need to fake this conversation. I got a text from my dad to make sure the cupcakes were submitted for order. Guess I'll see you tomorrow night."

The doors open, and he steps out with his hands in his pocket and heads towards the exit doors of the building.

I continue to my car and go join my favorite ladies at the spa.

After our relaxing and very much-needed day at the spa, I take my family out for dinner at Wollensky's Grill. Not only is the food amazing, but the views of the river at night are spectacular. I need a pick-me-up after the fire-starter week I've had. I made the reservations as we were getting dressed after our massages. The host seats us immediately, and I order a bottle of wine for the table.

"Thank you for such a wonderful day, Monie," Gwen says before taking a sip of her drink.

"Yes. Thank you. I enjoyed the spa. I'll have to get Marv to bring me when we go on vacation," Bev chimes in.

I do love when the whole tribe is together. We have lots of fun. Aunts, uncles, cousins, Mom, and what used to be Dad. But since their divorce, he's moved on to a new life. I wonder if that's why my mom is marrying so soon.

"Now, Nina, why are you marrying this man after only a month of courtship? One of those weeks were on a cruise." Aunt Beverly took my thoughts and formed the perfect question.

All eyes turn to my mother who looks a bit upset but seemingly feels she needs to answer in a diplomatic way.

"To be honest, like we told the kids, we aren't getting younger. There is no need for a long dating period when you are our age. We really enjoyed each other's company on the boat, and when we got back on land, we spent two weeks in Miami before returning home."

"He has a child?" Aunt Gwen asks.

"Oh, yes. He and Monie work together. It was a real shocker. I mean, who would've guessed this world was so small."

"Aww, she's getting the brother you and Albert never had," Aunt Bev pokes fun.

They all cackle, and internally I want to hurl. My facial expression clearly indicates I'm not amused.

"Oh, I see she didn't like the joke. Well, it doesn't matter. As long as you're happy, Nina. The one thing that counts. To my baby sister, Nina Richelle Hodge-Greene, soon-to-be Weathers. I hope you two find happiness to last eternal," Beverly toasts my mother, and we join in. After-all, her happiness is the sole thing that matters. Looking at her smile while those three carry on is worth being related to *him*.

"So will my uncles George and Marv be joining the festivities?" I ask, interrupting their little girls' gathering which completely nullifies my existence.

"Yes, love. Why you ask?" Gwen answers with a question.

"They're not here now, so I was wondering if I'd see them."

"Oh no, dear. We wanted to come in early to spend some time with you two and check out this fella who's marrying our sister. You know we have to give him the once-over."

"So, have you met him yet?"

"Well, we saw him on your mother's phone. He video called her when we got to your house. He is a devilishly handsome man. We didn't know he had kids."

"Kid," I interject. "I mean. he only has one child, Lucas."

They all look at me with raised eyebrows.

"Monie, do you not like Lucas?" my mother asks, taking my hand into hers.

Suddenly the conversation, or rather, the chewing out from earlier, replays in my mind, and I feel some type of way. If I tell her yes, we don't get along and we were faking it on Saturday, not only will it be a lie, but it would put a kink in her happiness.

"No, Mom. We get along fine. Work is where we have conflict sometimes."

"Good. Because even though I love Charles, I have to make sure my little princess is okay with the entire package."

She caresses my face the way only a mother does, and

although I like it, the pit of my stomach knots up when I hear that word again: *princess.*

"Well, isn't this table full of beautiful women. I especially like this one here." Charles leans in and gives my mother a kiss on the lips, in front of me.

I roll my eyes and down my drink when I see his son is also in tow. I look different than when he last saw me. I have my hair up in a bun, and I'm wearing white shorts and heeled sandals, and a navy blue, off-the-shoulder shirt with no bra.

"Good evening, everyone," Lucas says, greeting the table. "Simone," he adds, his tone clipped.

"Hi, Lucas. So lovely to see you this evening." This hurts me to fake more than you know, but I must keep up appearances.

I stand to change seats, offering Mr. Weathers mine so he can sit next to my mother. Lucas takes a seat between my two aunts.

"So how was the spa?" Mr. Weathers asks.

"Oh, it was so nice. Monie went all out for us. Complete with massages, facials, mani-pedis. The whole shebang. My little girl loves to spoil her mother and aunts. Ever since she got this job, she always makes sure we have trips and time to spend with each other. I think it's because she never had a sibling."

"Well, now she has this handsome brother." My aunt takes her hands and squeezes his cheeks together. "If anything, she'll be kicking ass to keep the girls off him."

The whole table erupts in laughter, minus the subjects being discussed.

I take in a deep breath, and as I exhale, Lucas looks at me with heat in his eyes. I go to brush my hair behind my ear and fail since it's all pinned up. "Excuse me, for a moment." I stand.

"Oh, look at what you did, Bev, you embarrassed Monie," My mother says when I leave.

The squabbling begins, and I can't wait to go outside. I open the door to the patio and watch the tour boat go by when I find a place against the rails of the deck. I take in the night air and try to figure out what the fuck is wrong with me. Too many things are rattling around in my head. Most of it is foreign, you know, stuff I've never dealt with. Like being called a princess, and it has two different meanings. Why do I get hot when Lucas gives me a certain look? Did I fuck myself out of the promotion? Am I being petty? I let the thoughts go round and round inside my mental space.

"Here, I thought you could use this." A hand appears with a glass of wine.

"Thanks, Lucas," I reply when I see it's him. "Sorry about my aunts."

"Don't be. They're sweet. They said, 'Here, look at these pictures of your new sister' before pulling out the photo album they had uploaded onto their cloud. You were an adorable little girl."

"Oh God. The photo album? I did that for them as a

gift one Christmas in case the real ones were lost. Great. You saw the one where I was naked in the tub, too, didn't you?"

"Yeah. But what child doesn't have one of those?" He takes a pull from his glass with a smile on his lips.

I feel compelled to speak to him, but seeing how things went at the office, I may not be the person he wants to speak with. I go to open my mouth when his phone rings.

"Hello," he answers. His face beams listening to the other person speak.

I can tell it's the same female voice, and it adds to the confusion in my head. I immediately think it's Mandy from work and wonder *Why do I care?*

He walks away laughing, leaving me hanging.

I take my glass and go back to the table. "Hi, family. Sorry, I couldn't take the forthcoming baby stories, so I left ahead of them." I giggle.

"Where is Lucas?"

"I dumped his body in the river." I take a bite of my food.

They all turn and look at me with crazy eyes when I don't crack a smile at my joke. Little do they know, it could've very well been true.

"Sorry about that. I had to take a call. I went looking for my little sister and figured she must've wandered back inside to our loving parents," Lucas says as he rejoins us.

I roll my eyes externally, but internally I smile.

"I do have to go, so, Dad, put this on my card and I'll tell our server to box mine. Can you bring it home for me?"

"Sure, son. I guess you are going on a late date with that young lady from the weekend you were telling me about."

"I have a date, but it's not with her." Lucas looks at me.

"Oh, a player. Well, I'm sure Monie will have a talk with you about your ways," my mom adds. "She doesn't like men who play the field."

Meanwhile, my throat catches a lump, and I fight hard to hold back my tears. Even going as far as to fake a sneeze so the drops that did pool could fall.

"Achoo!" I wipe the falling droplets of water and grab my napkin to wipe them.

"Oh dear, are you getting sick?" my aunty asks.

"No, ma'am, my allergies, I'm sure.

"Well, you ladies have a lovely evening." Luke kisses my mom and aunties on their cheeks. "It was a pleasure meeting you both."

"Likewise," Aunt Gwen says as she bats her eyelashes.

"Dad see you when I get home. Bye, sis."

Lucas strolls out of the restaurant, and my heart sinks even more.

We finish our meal with light conversation and third-degree questioning by Gwen and Bev. The server brings the bill, and I take it from him.

"I got it," I boast proudly.

"But Lucas said for me to put it on his card."

"Now, dear, don't get in between Monie and her motives. I'm sure she is only trying to one-up your son."

"Our son come Friday." He kisses my mom, and it's not one I want to see any parents engage in. It's deep, sensual, and yucky.

"Ready to go, ladies?" I interrupt the slow-simmering show of affection.

"I guess our daughter is ready to go home. I'll talk to you later after she goes to bed. I don't want her to hear what you do to me on those video calls," my mom says.

"That's it. I'll meet y'all at the car." I grab my small purse and head out to the valet station to get my vehicle and see Lucas come back.

"Fast date?" I say when I approach his car.

He didn't see me at first since his eyes were focused on my legs as I walked towards him.

"Dad called and said he was ready, and I didn't want him to take an Uber back to my place."

"So, what happened on your date?"

He diverts his eyes away, obviously dodging the question before turning back to respond.

"Simone, I owe you an apology for the way I acted today. I was so—"

"Son, you're here. I hope I didn't spoil your evening."

"No, sir. Everything went as I had hoped it would."

"Well, goodnight, my dear. See you Friday." His dad gives me a hug and climbs into the passenger seat of Lucas' car.

The valet brings my car up and hands me the keys. "Here you go, miss."

I tip him and enter my vehicle and buckle up. The Weathers pull off, and when my family settles, we go home.

CHAPTER NINE

Since we all inadvertently met up on Wednesday, there was no need for a pre-wedding dinner. Instead, we run errands, gather decorations, make calls to the DJ and party rental company, and confirm my aunties have all they need. I went over to the Hilton and paid for two suites for when my uncles arrive. Since my place is the focal point of the ceremony/reception, the place will be crawling with people left and right.

For a small intimate gathering, this is turning into a big event. Close friends and family and their plus-ones quickly turned into a party for sixty. After listening to my aunts argue over not having enough food to support the reception, I called a caterer for reinforcement and added an extra refrigerator to help store all the food which should be delivered soon.

Lucas and his dad had to pitch in and help with grabbing the linens for the tables, the faux trees, and gazebo. Even though I'm still mad and hurt, I manage to keep those feelings bottled up for the sake of our parents. I look around at the magic unfolding and realize my mom was right. This is beautiful.

"We need to do a dry run," mom says as she walks through holding the hand of her soon-to-be Mister.

"Mom, both of you have been married before. Why do we need a mock-up?"

"Charles and I were talking, and we both don't know how we are to enter into the wedding or if we will be introduced as the Mr. and Mrs. in a grand fashion for the reception."

I think about what she is saying, and it makes sense.

"Come on, son, let's go and get in place."

We all head inside and stand near the makeshift trellis they erected in my open living room. My uncle agreed to step in as the minister.

"Dearly beloved..."

"We are gathered here today to get through this thing called life," Lucas and I both say at the same time.

Our parents aren't happy.

"Sorry, Uncle Marv. Please continue."

"As I said, we are gathered here to witness the union between this man and this woman into holy matrimony."

He continues through the faux process, and my mind wanders to the past weekend. Friday night's inebriated sex, to Saturday's all-nighter with a little bit of sleep and a getting-to-know-you session. *I can't think about that right now.* I refocus and pay attention to the mock ceremony at hand.

"You may now kiss the bride," Marv announces.

The lovebirds go in for a kiss, and I'm not in the mood for PDA.

"Okay, now we've got that out of the way, we have hair appointments to get to, Mom." I gather my things while she runs to the room to do the same.

Aunt Gwen and Bev are heading to the hotel to rest and make sure their attire doesn't need any last-minute alterations.

"Hey, Simone," Lucas calls to me.

"Hey, Lucas," I say while going through my stack of mail before tucking it away. I look up and see him coming.

"Can I speak with you for a quick moment?"

"Sure, I have about ten minutes. What's up?" I keep it casual, so he doesn't know how he affects me. Last night while tossing and turning, I realized my developing feelings for him. Sure, usually you have these things then you fuck, but I think the anger I had masked those feelings all along.

"Lucas, baby. Hi," a lady calls out, and the voice sounds familiar. She's tall, blonde, with those trademark gray eyes. Tan skin and shapely.

"Aunt Rachel, you made it. So glad you could come."

They hug for a few minutes, and I realize that's the voice I heard through the phone.

"I couldn't miss my baby brother getting married. And who is this lovely woman? Is this your girlfriend?"

The red tinge of blush on his face and smile giveaway his embarrassment.

"No. Uh, this is actually my soon-to-be stepsister, Simone Greene. And, in a strange twist of things, my colleague."

"Oh, nice to meet you. I'm his aunt, Rachel. Well, I guess that will make me your aunt, too."

She takes me into a big hug, and I immediately feel the warmth of her spirit.

"It's nice to meet you. I'm sure my mother will be glad to know you're here. Let me go get her."

"Uh, actually, Simone. I really need to talk to you." He turns to his relative and speaks. "Dad is up those stairs and outside if you want to go surprise him."

He's being very cryptic, but I follow along. She takes off for the rooftop, and he shuttles me into the kitchen.

"Okay, Lucas. What's going on?"

"I don't want to fight anymore. This animosity between us has gone too far. So tonight, my place, dinner. Just the two of us so we can clear the air. Nothing else, I promise. I want to do this before the wedding tomorrow. I want to do this before the sunrises in the morning."

I start to say no, but it wouldn't be fair to either of us. Plus, he's right. Chances are we'll be seeing a lot more of each other after five PM tomorrow afternoon.

"Okay. Text me your address."

"Cool." He takes out his phone and sends me his location.

I stare at it for a few minutes and realize it's only fifteen minutes from me. "I didn't realize you were so close," I say when I put in his address to map.

"Yeah, well, I bought it for a great deal. Couldn't pass up the chance."

"Simone, I'm ready now. I met Charles' sister, and she is such a delight. We invited her to dinner tonight. I hope that's okay," my mother speaks upon entering the room.

"Mom, Lucas and I have to close out some business, so I'm going to have dinner at his place and skip dining out with the parents tonight. Plus, we have to finalize things for tomorrow."

"Makes sense. Well, come on, let's go get our wigs split."

I'll never get used to my mom trying to use modern terminology.

Lucas grabs my hand as I try to walk away. "Tonight?" he says, looking at me intently with those piercing gray eyes of his.

"See you at seven."

Lucas Weathers

Dinner's done, wine is chilling, and I think I'm about to

walk a hole into my oak hardwood floors, I think to myself. I've had women over here before, not that I'm a cad or anything of the sort, but the fact Simone is on her way up the elevator has me nervous. Tonight will be the defining moment of what will or will not become of us moving forward. I plan to lay it all on the line, after we clear the air. I thought I made my intentions clear, but since the staffing change at work on Monday and our blowup in front of everyone on Tuesday, I didn't know what would happen. I knew nothing was going on between her and Edwards, I was in my feelings. I wasn't happy about being offered the position over her, and when I tried to explain it, she didn't give me the chance. So, I was like fine, fuck it. It was the wrong way to handle things.

A knock at the door breaks my inner thoughts, and I rush to answer, buying myself a few moments to relax before swinging the entrance open.

"Hey, Simone," is all I can muster. She's breathtaking. Her hair is styled for tomorrow's event, but the spirals frame her beautiful face.

"Hi, Lucas."

"Come in. Make yourself at home." I step to the side, and she enters. The scent of her perfume is totally throwing me off my plan. "Would you like something to drink? I have wine or water if you're not drinking."

"Oh, no. I'm drinking. I just spent three hours at the hair salon with my mom and my aunts, who joined us shortly after we got there. They had me listening to things I wouldn't tell my plants."

She laughs, and my heart skips a beat and the sound. Even when she's being mean, I still want her. In fact, I want her more.

"That bad, huh?" I comment, handing her a glass of Cabernet.

"Let me put it to you like this: If you thought I was embarrassed at dinner Wednesday night, you would've thought I died today." She takes another sip and licks her lips in delight at the dark tones of the beverage.

I cautiously think about what her tongue and mouth do before pulling my thoughts back to reality. "Simone, I asked you here as sort of a truce."

"Yeah, I've been thinking about that. Actually, I haven't been able to sleep well because of it."

"Oh?" I haven't been able to sleep either because the taste of her kisses and pussy haunt me daily.

"I feel bad I turned sour with you after Armstrong made the announcement. I know you wouldn't do me like that. Especially after the weekend we had." She turns away when she mentions our time together.

The timer goes off interrupting my thoughts.

"Excuse me for a moment." I jog to the kitchen to take the dessert I bought out of the oven.

"What did you make?" she asks, approaching the kitchen.

"I really didn't have time to prepare, but I managed to

make roasted chicken with steamed veggies. The dessert is the only thing purchased."

"So, you cook? Like, for real?"

"Yeah. Remember we were gonna have dinner together Monday, but..."

"Again, I'm sorry."

"Why don't you go freshen up and let's eat. Leave all the bad stuff behind us. Truce?" I hold out my hand in true hatchet-burying fashion.

"Truce." She takes my hand, and I hold it a little longer than I should.

I stare into her eyes and I know what I was looking for is there. I decide to take a chance and lean in for a kiss. Surprisingly, she doesn't back away. I start with a soft peck before searching her face for a response. She smiles, and I go in for a longer, deep kiss.

"I've never been forgiven like that," she quips.

"Me either. Now we eat."

"Okay. Where's your bathroom?" she inquires.

"Oh, down the hall, first door on the right."

"Be right back."

As soon as she's out of earshot and view, I do a little victory jump. I prayed the evening would go like this, and it has. I serve up our meal and place the plates on the table. The click-clacking of her sandals walking back towards the room, alerts me to her return.

"I'm ready. I kept thinking about the menu while I was washing my hands." She giggles.

I pull the chair out and urge her to have a seat, then scoot her in.

"Wow, this looks amazing."

"Thanks. I learned to cook after my mom passed so I could keep part of her memories with me and Dad."

I look over. and her eyes fill with emotion.

She reaches out and covers my hand with hers. "You don't have to talk about it if you don't want. I didn't mean to bring up painful memories."

"Oh, I'm okay. But thanks." I retract my hand and take a bite of food.

She does the same, and I watch for the first reaction.

"Wow, this is so good," she mutters through a full mouth.

I know she went to finishing school and has manners, but I love it when she's just being her. She takes another stab at her food, and I watch in delight seeing her eyes roll for the second time. Come to think of it, I've seen that look before.

We complete our meal and talk about her day at the salon with her family over a glass of wine.

"Oh my god. Mom kept going on about her playlist. She has to have 'this' song played for 'this' moment, and my aunts kept objecting as to why she shouldn't play said song. It was horrible."

Simone is taking the brunt of the wedding planning, and I feel bad. She kneads her neck with her hands as she describes her afternoon outing.

I go stand behind the chair and massage her shoulders. I already know she responds well to my touch.

"Mmm, that's exactly what I need, Lucas. A good massage." Her head falls forward, allowing me to move a little farther down her neck and shoulders. "Mmm," she moans...again.

This is turning me on, and I try to shift a little to ease my excitement, until she leans her head back and whimpers. Now I'm as hard as the marble countertop. I remove my hands and step back, hoping some of the blood will drain from my dick.

"Why don't you turn to the side so I can have better access to massage your neck?" I suggest, buying me some time to will my hard-on away.

She follows through with the recommendation, and I go back to having a semi-mini. I apply pressure to the spine part of her neck and work across her shoulders, rubbing one side and then the next.

"Damn, I didn't realize how tense I was. That feels really good." She allows her head to fall forward, and I apply a little more pressure.

My full-on arousal returns as I listen to her approval of my fingers relaxing her muscles.

She accidentally brushes against my junk when she raises her head to an upright position. "Ooo, and here I thought you just wanted to give me a massage. Feels like you're enjoying this too," she says wittily.

Of course, I enjoy touching her, but it's not my only

reason for inviting her over. She stands and turns towards my direction, her gaze roaming over me, telling me it's okay, calling to and pleading for me not to pull away. I move the chair and take her mouth with mine. It could be my imagination, but her kisses taste sweeter.

She moans through our action, and I know she wants this moment as much as I do. Her arms snake around my neck, and I place my hands on her hips, walking her towards my bedroom. When we cross the threshold, she begins to undress, and I stop her.

"Simone, I don't want this to be only a sexual thing, two people sneaking around. I want to make a commitment to you."

Those may not be the words she wants to hear, but I had to let her know how I feel. I always told myself if given the opportunity, I wouldn't let her go.

"How? How would we do this? Our parents are getting married in less than twenty-four hours. What, do we sneak around for as long as this works?"

"Is this something you'd want?"

She takes a seat on the chair in my room. "Lucas, I think—no, I *know*—I've always had a liking for you. My drive to be the best at work only to have it overshadowed by you getting the clients I wanted, made it change from like to..."

"Hate?" I interject.

She glares at me. "Disgust. I mean, you walk around the office, and still do, by the way, like you are royalty, the king of account managers. When we let our egos get the best of us instead of forming a super team, neither of us got the software account. But you did get the senior position, and I felt some kind of way."

"I can call Armstrong right now and turn it down if you want."

"No, silly. Don't do that. I realize how bratty I was when I wasn't selected, and I took it out on you. Hearing my family refer to me as a princess only reminded me how I truly act, and you were right."

The erection has deflated as the conversation returns to clearing the air. "And now?" I say, taking a seat on the edge of my bed next to her. "What are you feeling?"

She takes a deep breath, grasping my hand into her palms, looking to me with those deep-brown, almond-shaped eyes. "Now I feel something deep for you, especially after this weekend, even though it was spent mainly in the bed."

"On the couch," I add.

"The floor," she retorts.

"Storage room."

We both giggle when we reminisce about our erotic time together.

I look at her smile, and it warms my insides. The way she bites her lip returns the blood to my formerly deflated dick.

"Anyway, I discovered an attraction to you, and I realize

I masked my emotions instead of speaking on them. Partly it was the risk of being rejected, especially with the grapevine saying you were with someone, so I knew then all bets were off. The only other thing was to reverse my feelings."

"You still didn't answer the question?"

"What?"

"Is this something you want?"

The quiet reserve that falls on her face lets me know she is thinking about the situation. Not in a how-do-I-let-him-down thought, but weighing the pros and cons.

Instead of letting her wonder any longer, I offer a compromise. "This seems like it would be a major decision for you. I know where I stand, but I don't want any pressure on you. So how about you come over here and we talk. Any subject you want."

She wrinkles her nose and smiles. "Like twenty-one questions kinda talk?"

"Sure. I'm game. Are you?"

She takes off her shoes and moves to the head of the bed and beckons me to join her with a few pats on the mattress.

I remove my socks and join her, snatching a pillow to prop behind my head.

She grabs one for comfort but looks at my feet with an awkward glare. "You have surprisingly attractive feet for a guy."

"Wow, sexist much?"

"I'm serious. Most men lack in the foot care area. Do you get a pedicure?"

"I'm not answering," I say, shaking my head.

"You have to. It's my first question."

"So, you are wanting to lead with that?"

"Yes. Now tell me." She gently and playfully pushes my arm.

"I do on occasion, but I generally do them myself. A friend taught me how in order to save money."

"Was it a girl you were seeing?"

"Do I get to ask any questions?"

"Yep. As soon as you answer the one on the floor."

"No, it wasn't. Well, not exactly. We went out, but it wasn't a serious thing. No sex, and no, not even a kiss before you follow up and ask. Now, my turn. When was your last serious romance?"

She yawns and deliberates for a minute.

"Hmm. I would have to say my sophomore year in college."

With a raised brow, I analyze and do the math in my head. "Simone, that's almost eight years."

"Mmhmm. I grew tired of dating. I really wanted to excel in life, not in love. I figured it would find me when it was ready, or I wasn't meant to have a relationship."

"That's a very positive outlook. Wish I had concentrated like you. I dated all through my school years, when I was old enough. Started with the sixth grade dance. But I could never find someone who rivaled me. Until..." Her quiet yet steady breathing catches my attention. I look over and see she has fallen asleep. I remember we were talking after sex Saturday night and she admitted once she gets comfortable, it's lights out. I pull the blanket over her, and she turns towards me, resting her head on my chest. And at that moment, I know her answer. Now we need to figure out how.

CHAPTER TEN

The sound of the door closing awakens me, and I realize I fell asleep in Lucas' bed, clothed and untouched. Last thing I remember is him talking about a middle school dance he attended. It doesn't take long for me to pass out. Highly intense moments that are diffused by alcohol, sex, or massages render me useless and unconscious.

"Lucas," I whisper as I push on him slightly. The sight of his bedside clock illuminates three-thirty-six AM. *Shit,* I think to myself.

"Lucas," I try again.

This time he stirs and puts his arm across his forehead.

"Someone came in," I say.

"Probably my dad. Come on, lie back down." He pats his chest, signaling where he wants me to be.

I wait for a few minutes to see if he will need a more direct nudge.

He soon springs upright. "Fuck, Simone! Uh, uh, I'm sorry. I should've taken you home instead of lying with you. Now we gotta sneak you out of here."

"Yes. This is precisely what I don't want to do," I retort. I grab my sandals, so they don't make a sound against his hardwood floors. I can't help but notice his facial expression is a bit saddened. Maybe it's because we didn't get to the sex part. Maybe it's for the best.

"Son, are you still up?" his dad calls from the other side of the door.

I scramble to my feet and hide away in his closet.

"Yeah, Dad. Come on in."

I cower to the floor amongst all his suits and dress attire neatly hanging on one side and his casual wear on the other. He has two magnificent built-in shoe shelves, one for dress and one for athletic. He even owns a few pairs of very expensive cowboy boots. I turn my attention back to the conversation on the other side of the door, not because I'm nosey, but to make sure there are no cues about opening the closet.

"Why are you up, son?"

"Oh, I um, heard you come in. So, how was the evening?"

"It was good, son. Real good. Rach told me what you did to get her here. I wanted to say thank you, again. Did you and Monie get everything finalized last night? The wedding is in fourteen hours and fifteen minutes."

"Most of it we got squared away. There's still an outstanding question I had, and she's going to look into it." His voice softens, and I know it has to do with the fact I never answered him.

"Well, that young lady has a great head on her shoulders. Did you know she spends two weekends out of the year renting out hotel suites for girls in a group home and giving them a Princess Party?"

"No, I didn't know."

"Son, for you two to work together, you sure know little about each other."

"Well, we kinda have this not-so-friendly work relationship."

"Ah, I see. Well, maybe you two should bury the hatchet. Put all the animosity behind you like me and Rachel did when your mother died. It makes out for a better relationship."

He doesn't know, but hearing those words makes me realize I've been holding on to my fake feelings for too long. Time for me to face the truth about Lucas.

"Goodnight, Dad. See you in a few hours for breakfast," Lucas says.

The door fastens, and after a few minutes, the closet doors swing open.

"Okay. You have about five minutes to get out before he comes back out of his room.

"How do you know he will?"

"He always undresses then goes to the bathroom before turning in."

"Oh. Well, I wanted to talk with you for a second. Maybe we can get a few minutes before the ceremony starts."

"Okay. Let me walk you out."

We tiptoe down the hall to the living room where he opens the door.

"Well, thank you for dinner and a lovely evening. I'll text you to let you know I made it home."

"Okay. Goodnight."

"Good morning." I reach up to give him a peck on his cheek, but he turns his head, and our lips meet instead. The kiss is a slow simmer. I drop my purse and rest my hands upon his shoulders. He finds my waist, and his hands apply gentle pressure when he pulls me into his space.

"Son, why are you outside?" his dad calls out.

I dart down the staircase to the first floor, exit the building, and enter my car to head home. I text Lucas when I walk through my front door.

"My, you were out late, missy," my mom says as she wakes from the couch.

"Mom, why are you on the couch? You should be in your bed."

"Oh, Charles and I watched a few movies till he went

home, and I wanted to wait on my baby. Where were you?"

"I was out with my friends chatting over wine. I should've called."

"No problem, baby. I knew you were okay. You've done a lot over the past week and you deserve to relax. Did you and Lucas get all the details worked out?"

"Yes, ma'am. We got the final details done, and the ceremony will be beautiful. No surprises on my watch."

"I can't believe you've worked with Lucas and never mentioned him during our calls."

"We don't exactly have a friendly work relationship. We're sorta rivals."

"That explains a lot. You two never spoke about work much or even to each other when we were all together, and you seemed cold to him."

"True, however, we squashed all the beef between us and buried it for the sake of a new union. And if I don't get any sleep, I will have circles under my eyes and the makeup artist will have a lot to work out tomorrow. Goodnight, Mother."

She stands from her sitting position and embraces me in a tight, warm and loving manner. "Good morning, my little princess."

I saunter off to my room to squeeze in as much sleep as possible.

The florist arrived on schedule as their company promises. Too bad I wasn't up to greet them. In all my years, I've never slept through an alarm until today—the biggest day of my mother's life, since I was born, of course. I stumble out of bed when my mom yells my name for the umpteenth time, using first, middle, and last name. I struggle to find my way to the bathroom so I can wash my face, brush my teeth, and join in the preparations. When I enter my living room, moms doing her best to direct traffic, but I can tell she's frustrated.

"Mom, I got it. I'm sorry I overslept."

"It's okay, Monie. All that matters is you're here now, so get busy." She exits to her room to begin her preparations, and I am left to untangle this mess.

After a few redirects, the flowers are finally getting in place. I hand the florist a walkie-talkie to reach me in case they have questions as they finish the arrangements and setting up the arch for the inside. I borrow two of the florist staff, and we go meet the party rental team on the rooftop for the red-carpet setup we are using to announce the new Mr. and Mrs. and the installation of the makeshift dance floor. Once I have all those jobs going, I redirect my attention to the buffet area which was set up last night and make sure the extra refrigerator is still running. When I open it, the cool air from inside is a welcome change.

"Ahh," I exhale aloud. I don't care who hears me. It's the opening of summer, and I swear we've been in it for about three weeks. At eleven AM, it should not be this hot.

"You could go back inside to cool off," a voice says behind me.

I think it's a worker being kind—and nosey, mind you—but my eyes widen when I turn to speak.

"Lucas. What are you doing here so early?"

His smile widens, and I realize I'm not dressed or even made up. Not even a little. I fumble with my headscarf and cross my arms in a self-conscious manner.

"Oh, I had to drop off a few things for the refreshments, remember?"

"Oh yeah, the liquor and beer. Thank you again. I totally spaced on that detail."

He outstretches his hand and allows his fingers to gently brush against my already heated skin, which his touch makes it even hotter. "No problem. You've had a crazy week."

I look at him and smile at his response. I go to speak but the walkie beeps.

"Ms. Greene, we have a small situation and we need your assistance."

"Okay, I'll be right in."

"Simone, do you need me to do the bar setup while I'm here? I have about an hour before I have to go home and get ready."

"Shit, an hour? Is that where we are on time?"

"Calm down. We have about four hours since it begins at five, but Dad and I are going to the cemetery first, then getting dressed for the ceremony before we go pick up Aunt Rachel."

"Oh. Okay. Whew, I thought I was horribly off schedule. If you want, you can set it up. The tent covers and misting fans are on their way, so hopefully we'll have a nice and comfy, yet cool reception."

He begins to unpack the libations and stock the fridge. "You planned a nice event for such short notice," he says, continuing to stow away to beverages.

"Well, our parents gave us their want list, and we made sure it happened." I chuckle a bit and then recover. "Anyway, I'll see you later, I guess. I mean, we are standing as the witnesses."

"True. See you later, sis."

"Right back atcha, bro."

We laugh as I turn away and head back inside to see what fire is simmering with the florist.

4:55 PM

The guests have all arrived and are patiently waiting for the start of the ceremony. Mom and I are being blessed by the pastor before the start of her new life as Mrs. Nina Weathers. Once he completes his prayer, he heads out to the arch where the two will be joined as one. Tears well when I see the happy glow across my mother's face. Her smile only highlights the twinkle in her light-brown eyes.

She looks to me and holds out her hand. "Come here, Monie."

I dab the droplets of happiness and take her palm.

"My only wish is you find someone who makes you feel the way Charles makes me feel. I know you don't want to talk about it, and we're not, but I wanted to let you know what your father and I had was special. But our fire died out, baby, and I had to move on with my life like he did. It's not usually how love goes, so don't be afraid to take chances for fear it will end up like ours did. Okay?" She tilts my face up, her eyes searching for understanding.

"Yes, ma'am." I pull her into an embrace and fight back the tears threatening to ruin my makeup Sasha spent an hour applying, then touching up in-between photos.

We part, and she smiles when she hears the music signaling our entrance.

"Time to get hitched," she comments.

We hold hands till we enter the hallway.

"I love you, Mom, and I'm so happy for you." I place a kiss on her cheek before I take the first step into the living area.

I walk down the small makeshift aisle, peering at the small crowd before us. Faces familiar and not. There is one I see standing beside his dad at the altar. The way that suit hugs his body reminds me of how my legs seemingly melted to his waist. Clinging to every inch of his body as he moved slowly in and out of my pussy. His gray eyes light a path of desire within me when our gazes lock. His smile sends me over the edge, and I nearly stumble approaching my assigned position. *Control yourself, missy,* I think internally. I clear my throat and turn to see mother walking up to her spot. She and Mr. Weathers join hands, and the beginning starts now.

"Welcome! Charles and Nina have brought us together here for an occasion of great joy and a cause for great celebration. They have chosen each one of you to be here with them to witness their wedding vows as they join as husband and wife."

The officiant begins the service, and I marvel at the couple, taking notice of the wrinkles by their eyes and around their lips as they smile lovingly at one another. My gaze drifts off to Lucas and he glances up and catches me in my gaze daze. The words being spoken become distant while the memories of the past week flood my mind. The good, the bad, and the unanswered. I can't see him the same any longer. The dynamic has certainly changed, and now things are becoming even more awkward with the marriage taking place right before us.

"The time has come to exchange the rings, and the couple will recite their vows together," the officiant says.

We both pass the rings to our parents, and they turn towards each other and speak the following:

"God and the universe have given us a second chance at happiness. I come today to give you my love, to give you my heart and my hope for our future together. I promise to bring you joy, to be at home with your spirit and to learn to love you more each day, through all the days of our lives. My love for you is endless and eternal," they both recite.

"Charles and Nina, you have come here today of your own free will, and in the presence of family and friends, have declared your love and commitment to each other. You have given and received a ring as a symbol of your promises. By the power of your love and commitment to each other, and by the power vested in me, I now pronounce you husband and wife. Charles, you may now kiss your bride."

Charles takes my mother into a back-bending embrace and lays a romantic kiss on her.

"Friends and family, I now present to you the newly married couple. Let's hear it for 'em!"

Thunderous roars and claps erupt and the new Mr. and Mrs. turn to the crowd and hold their joined hands in the air. They walk down the aisle amongst well-wishers and stand over to the side to mingle. Lucas and I follow, him grabbing my hand as we stroll.

"This was a nice ceremony," he says.

I blush slightly feeling his gaze skim over my face. "It really was. I knew they were in love, but I didn't know how deep it was."

We both look to the happy couple and can't help but share in their joy.

"Well, I guess I'll get upstairs and make sure everything is ready for the reception. Would you mind making the announcement?"

"Uh, sure. I can do that. I'll see you on the rooftop." He grabs one of the cordless mics and announces the reception will begin in fifteen minutes.

I make a quick check of the food, drinks, and see if the DJ is ready with the playlist, then signal to Lucas to send the guests on up. Lucas enters the area escorting my aunts while my uncles chaperone his Aunt Rachel. I hand them each a glass of their pre-selected beverage and follow through with a drink of my own.

"Ladies and gentlemen, introducing the couple of the hour, Mr. and Mrs. Charles Weathers," the DJ announces the arrival, and the bubble machine shoots out sentiments of joy as they walk through them to the dance floor. "The couple will have their first dance as husband and wife."

Perfect by Ed Sheeran plays, and I can't help but tear up watching them dance. From the little pecks of affection they share with one another to the twinkle in their eyes under the stringed lights and the glow of the rising moon, I couldn't imagine a moment more perfect. I'm so engaged in them, I don't see when Lucas appears beside me.

"Hey," he says in a breathy tone.

"Hey," I reply in sniffles. "Have you ever seen something so beautiful?" I continue.

"Actually, I have. I'm looking at her right now."

I turn and give him the once-over when he takes my hand and leads me to the dance floor.

"Lucas, what are you doing?" I query. I glance around

and see everyone ogling us as he pulls me in to a close embrace and sways to the music.

"I'm staking my claim in my girl."

"Yours? But our parents just got..."

"I don't care. I'm not going to let this opportunity get away." He tilts my head up towards his, and with his hands placed firmly on either side of my face, he leans in and kisses me. His tongue breaks through, and I reciprocate while his hands move to my waist as I wrap mine around his neck. And for a brief moment I forget where I am. The music, the air, this man, all combined, have me in a state of bliss.

"Nina, do you see this?" Mr. Weathers says to my mother as they stand by us.

"Yes, Charles, I do. And I have never seen my baby so happy."

I rest my head against Lucas' chest, and we continue to dance, and at this moment, I know I am falling for my rival.

Did you enjoy Rivals? Join my email list for alerts of future stories and sneak peaks.

www.mlpreston.com/where-to-get-the-goods

ABOUT THE AUTHOR

ML Preston, was born and raised in Oklahoma City. An avid and voracious reader, she was encouraged to nurture her active imagination and quickly found a passion for storytelling. She spins sagas of passion and romance where the lines between race and creed, physical perfection and social norms disappear in the face of love. Novels of real love; erotic connections with a heart and soul that everyone can relate. She makes a home in Texas with her husband and three children, who keep her grounded when the voices call on her to tell their story. And they never stop calling.

Website:
www.mlpreston.com

Facebook:
www.facebook.com/PrestonML

Instagram:
instagram.com/author_ml_preston

OTHER TITLES

Unthinkable
Untouchable
Unbreakable
Love Lessons
High Roller
Road Block (Escape Series #22)
The Designer
Southern Charm

UPCOMING RELEASES 2020*

Rivals
Crash
Detour (Escape Series #34)
All-In (Aces & Eights Series)
Falling For the Rock Star

*Release Date TBD

Made in the USA
Columbia, SC
07 June 2022